Cleopatra
Queen of Egypt

Cleopatra
Queen of Egypt

A BIOGRAPHICAL NOVEL

Dorothy Cowlin

WAYLAND · LONDON

First published in Great Britain (1970)
by Wayland (Publishers) Ltd
101 Gray's Inn Road London WC1

© Dorothy Cowlin (1970)

SBN 85340 004 0

MADE AND PRINTED IN GREAT BRITAIN BY
THE GARDEN CITY PRESS LIMITED,
LETCHWORTH, HERTFORDSHIRE

Cleopatra
Queen of Egypt

CONTENTS

7

1 A Pharaoh's Throne

CLEOPATRA became conscious of the smell of burning oil. She lay for a second or two longer, sniffing and identifying this, then opened her eyes.

Kararea, one of her father's slaves, was standing beside her bed, looking silently down at her. She was carrying a lamp, lifted so as to throw the light on to Cleopatra's face, and so waken her.

"What, Kararea? What's the matter?" cried Cleopatra sharply. There was something alarming in the woman's silence, and in her expression.

"Your father's asking for you. He's ill! Thinks he's dying!" said the woman bleakly.

"Oh! And *is* he?" cried Cleopatra, jumping up and throwing on a wrap.

"Only the gods can tell us that, my lady!" said Kararea, without the faintest pretence of grief. That was not to be expected of course, for Ptolemy, as Cleopatra well knew, was not a kind master to his servants.

There were crowds of people in the ante-room, including (ominously enough) a little bevy of professional mourners in full-dress. The royal bedroom too was thick with people: priests galore of course, officials of many degrees, three physicians, and, at the foot of the bed, Cleopatra's two young brothers, and her sister Arsinoe, putting on an act as usual, whimpering and dabbing at her tearless eyes, the little crocodile! Everybody else simply stood about in silence, with an air of eager expectancy.

9

Cleopatra saw at once that this was no false alarm. Her father was not at any time a pretty sight, particularly in bed in the middle of the night. But she thought that she had never seen anything quite so hideous, and yet so pathetic, as the face that was turned up to hers as she approached the bed.

"Cleopatra?" he said, peering at her through the greenish lamplight. His voice barely reached her ears, and with it came a little puff of warm, foul breath, reeking as usual with date-wine, onions, and all the drugs the doctors had poured into him. She turned her head away slightly, and silently pressed his sweaty hand.

"You're a good girl. Got brains. Best in the family.... Must've got'm from your mother ... couldn't have been *me*! ... I want, it is my last wish ... you are to inherit the throne ... jointly, you and your eldest brother, that's the best.... You two get wed ... like your mother and me before you.... Best way ... keep in the family...."

The breathy murmur lapsed. Suddenly his head lolled over on the greasy leather head cushion. A shadow, greenish yellow in colour like the belly of a frog, travelled quite rapidly over his face. The crowd stood silent.

Ptolemy XIII was dead, Cleopatra and Ptolemy XIV reigned in his place.

It was the traditional task of the priests and the embalmers to make ready the body of the dead Pharaoh for its journey to "the Country of the West". In their grotesque masks, shaped like the head of Anubis the dog and the god of the other world, these people busied themselves in the palace for some seventy days.

And certainly Ptolemy XIII looked the better for their labours, more dignified than he had for years. Wrapped round and round in funerary bandages, all the necessary little spells and amulets for his spiritual safety bound into place between the folds, his bulbous stomach deflated, smoothed into the flowing lines proper to a mummy, his bloated features encased in a mask of plaster, painted in the colours of his lost youth, he made quite a decent "Westerner".

How would he fare when it came to the weighing of his heart in the balance, against the feather of the goddess Truth, in that kingdom of the dead? Ptolemy XIII must surely have committed a high proportion of those forty-two sins of which one had to be proved innocent, to be accepted into the company of Osiris, the god of the dead?

He had certainly made a sad mess of things, so far as his own kingdom in this world was concerned.

"Auletes" ("the Flute Player") they had nicknamed him: a term of contempt, meaning that was all that he was good for. Not that there was any harm in playing a flute, in private, and as an amateur. But to do it in public, in the company of professionals and even in open competition with them—such low creatures, as everybody knows! It was so despicable. That's what the name was getting at, as well as his disgusting debaucheries

This sort of thing might have been forgiven, if he had only been an efficient ruler. As Pharaoh, it was his right, of course, to tax the people. But not so greedily that the poor wretches could barely make enough to eat. And then, on top of that, to alienate the priests by grabbing their land and revenues, and to imagine he could smooth them down by building that showy new temple at Dendyra, that had cost the earth—out of their own pockets!

No wonder he had been turned out of the country three years ago, and only been able to get back with the help of a Roman general. The country was still in debt to the Romans, to the tune of 17,500,000 drachmas, for that and other assistance.

Ah well, he was a Westerner now. Whatever his shortcomings as an earthly king, he was entitled to all the traditional rites and ceremonies of the Egyptian religion. Cleopatra saw that everything proper was done for him. And so, in due course, at the end of its seventy days' grooming, the corpse of Ptolemy XIII was solemnly conducted in a silver sarcophagus, engraved with hieroglyphic prayers, to its final resting-place in the temple of Serapis.

"INTEF," said Cleopatra, one morning shortly after the completion of these duties, "I want your advice."

This man Intef, scribe, scholar, priest in the temple of Ptah, had been giving her the benefit of his wisdom for as long as she could remember, ever since she was a little girl, and he her tutor. Through him it was that she had learned both to read and to speak the native Egyptian: the only member of her family who had taken the trouble to master this difficult language, ugly to the ear of the foreigner, with its clicks and glucks and bunches of consonants, but to her mind as comfortable-sounding as the quiet babbling of water on the underside of a boat on the Nile.

It was through Intef also that she had come to know something of the history of this incredibly ancient land. Many a tale had he told her of the times of King Khufu and King Khafra, the pyramid-makers; of King Pepi, who ruled until he was nearly a hundred years old; of King Thothmes, the mighty warrior, who had pushed out the boundaries of his empire eastwards to the river Euphrates and southwards far beyond the second cataract of the Nile.

That was very long ago of course, centuries ago. For many hundreds of years since then, Egypt's history had been of one humiliation after another, first at the hands of the Assyrians, then of the Persians, and finally the Macedonians.

"But, Intef, *I* am a Macedonian! *I* am one of these detestable Ptolemies!" she had once pointed out, when he had gone into one of his cursing bouts on this subject.

He came to a sudden halt, his mouth slowly spreading in a sheepish smile.

"You!" he said. "I forget sometimes that you are not one of

my own people. And in any case, you are to me simply my pupil, our princess, and the daughter of our Pharaoh."

Soaked in the past as he was, Intef was all there in the present too. Never once had she caught him out in even a whiff of treason against her father, though she knew pretty well what he must think of "the flute player". Intef and his daughter Charmion, who had been virtually brought up with her as a sister (far dearer indeed than her own blood-sister Arsinoe) were the nearest thing she had for friends. And without Intef to advise, how could she even contemplate her future as queen of this country?

So: "Intef!" she went on, "*Must* I marry my brother?"

He looked at her for a second before he answered. She thought she could detect a certain compassion in his dark, rather protuberant eyes, calm and gentle, but all alive with intelligence.

"It was your father's wish," he pointed out, after a moment, "and it is the custom, *has* been so, not only in your own family, but far back in our history, for sister and brother to marry, where there might otherwise be strife, harmful to the people."

"Oh—it's not because he's my *brother* that I mind. But— Intef—he's only ten! What in the world is the good of a brat of ten to a woman of eighteen?"

"He'll grow."

"Yes, uglier and nastier with every year. Intef, you *know* what a beastly little rat he is! You know he detests me, and I him. Oh, it's unthinkable!"

"The unthinkable sometimes has to be thought, in politics. Nobody ever imagined it would be a love-match. It is simply a matter of expediency. And don't you see, my dear girl, his very youthfulness is to your advantage. With any luck, you can make yourself virtually the sole ruler, from the start. And if there came to be any trouble, I think I may assure you the people would be on your side."

"Oh well—you may be right. I suppose I'd better go through

with it. But I can promise you this. It'll be a marriage on papyrus only. I'll not have that brat in *my* bed!"

And so Cleopatra and her little brother were duly crowned, Queen and Pharaoh, and man and wife.

It was all done in the proper traditional style, at the temple of Ptah in Memphis, correct to the last detail, including the "running forth of Apis", the sacred black bull of the temple. Apis in fact was far too old at this time to "run forth" in any real sense of the word. Decked with flowers and gilded ropes, he was simply *led* forth, meek as a cow, from the eastern door of his sacred stall, to join the coronation procession.

Ptolemy XIV created trouble from the beginning, by objecting to his wife being crowned with the "double crown of Upper and Lower Egypt". He wanted her to assume merely the head-dress of the "King's Chief Wife".

Cleopatra wasn't standing for that. "Or I might as well abdicate straight away," as she said to Intef. "I am joint Pharaoh, after all. My father wished it so. Otherwise what point is there in marrying the creature?"

So duplicates had to be made of all the royal insignia, the sacred crook, the flail, the sceptre, and the ancient crown that was more like a tall cap, with the coiled cobra on the forehead. Cleopatra went through the ceremony in the traditional male costume, slightly modified. And every item of ritual had to be done twice over, once for herself, once for her brother.

It was a long, wearisome affair, all in "the evil heat of the summer" as the saying was. Fans and awnings were powerless. The heat was like the coals of a brazier emptied repeatedly over one's head. Running with sweat, hundreds of shaven priestly pates, dipping and bobbing their homage, flashed like so many bronze mirrors in the sun.

The sweat ran down her own body too. Yet as Cleopatra walked from altar to altar, as she sat, and stood, and sat again, in her gold-laden apron and her jewel-laden collar, listening to the drone of the priests turning her from girl to goddess, there was a solemn thrill in the thought of the antiquity of it all. She could almost see before her, stretching away into the darkness of pre-history, a ghostly procession of other Pharaohs, walking like herself from altar to altar, clad in the same weighty garments, listening to the same immemorial and sacred drone.

A Pharaoh was required to make no vows. Oaths were for subjects to swear, to and by the name of the Pharaoh.

But within her own mind, Cleopatra made that day a solemn promise. She would rule well. She would try to go down on the walls of her tomb as a good Pharaoh to this land she loved so dearly. She would be as the mother-goddess Isis to these seven million people of the Two Lands of Egypt.

2 *In the shadow of Rome*

CLEOPATRA was only eighteen at her father's death, and though very well educated in some ways, thanks to Intef, had not been directly trained in the work of government.

In the course of the next three years she began to find out how limited was the actual scope of the "divine" Pharaoh.

Egypt was a bureaucracy, had been so for centuries. Long before her ancestor, the first Ptolemy, had come from Macedonia to take it over, a most elaborate and highly centralised system of government had been evolved, worked by a great network of civil servants.

In this vast piece of machinery the Pharaoh was merely one of the cog-wheels—though perhaps the largest one.

Take the Inundation Ceremonies, for instance.

If the Nile did not rise each year enough to spread its mud and waters over most of the cultivated land, the people of Egypt must starve. To ensure against such a catastrophe, it was the duty of the Pharaoh to go each year at a certain date to certain temples, to perform certain rituals, ending with the symbolic cutting of an earth-bridge, to allow water to flow into an irrigation canal.

"I suspect the Nile will please itself whether or not it rises!" Cleopatra remarked privately to Intef, after her first such ceremony. "Aren't there some philosophers who believe that the water comes from the mountains of Ethiopia, beyond my boundaries?"

"That is so. But the people believe otherwise. And there's more to it than that. The Nile may rise, but it must be controlled if it is to do us any good. Channels must be kept clear, new channels cut. Dams and dykes must be repaired. People have to work hard to do these things. It is your role to focus all this labour, as it were, like a burning glass. Otherwise, do you think it would be done?"

Not that Pharaoh was simply an idle figure-head. Far from it. There were quantities of monotonous, routine work to do. Papers to sign, letters to read and write, legal cases to decide, interviews with officials: her days were filled from dawn to sunset with such matters. Each night she went to her bed exhausted, yet feeling she had not shifted by one cog the life of one single subject out of its centuries-old groove.

The people were not as contented, she knew, as they should be under so well-intentioned a monarch as herself. The burden of taxes was enormous: back-breaking, so her Egyptian-speaking friends complained (and indeed plenty of her Greek citizens too).

It did seem to her outrageous that, for instance, a measure of olive oil should cost as much as 52 drachmas, of which 34 was collected in taxes. But financial experts all assured her that it was not possible to reduce the burden, and still pay for all the machinery of government.

Even such small reforms as she felt able to attempt were perpetually thwarted by her brother and co-ruler, young Ptolemy: or rather, by his hangers-on.

"The Rat" (as she always thought of him) was such a stupid little idiot. His tutors had never really taught him to read or write, even in his own language, let alone foreign ones. How could he converse with foreign ambassadors, or hope to understand state affairs? He wasn't even eager to learn. No—if it had been only a question of the Rat himself, she could have run rings round him.

But then there were these "advisers" of his, one or other of whom always insisted upon being present at business of state.

"*That* lot—advisers!" Cleopatra would scoff. "Why, they're little better than slaves! Photinus, the Eunuch, that used to be his male nurse, puffed up now into his Ratship's Chamberlain! And Theodotus, one-time Tutor, Secretary of State! Certainly he has *need* of a secretary, a nit-wit that can't even read or write!"

"Don't under-rate those two," Intef warned her, "they're not stupid, and *could* be dangerous."

"Oh I know. I don't trust them further than the tip of my ear. Nor that fellow Achillas either, clanking about the palace as if he were Hercules, and the sky would fall if he didn't hold it up! He, by the way, is a bit too thick just lately, for my peace of mind, with my dear sister! I've caught them in the corridors and the palace gardens, with their heads together in a manner that's hardly proper for a princess and a hired soldier, and isn't healthy for *me*. I sometimes wonder whether it wouldn't be a good plan to replace Achillas."

"I think the man might be more dangerous, deprived of his Command of the Palace Guards, than *with* it," objected Intef.

"I meant get rid of him, in the most final sense," said Cleopatra coolly.

Intef showed no sign of horror.

"It is sometimes necessary to remove an implacable adversary in that way," he agreed, "but not too often, my dear. And only when strictly necessary. We have no proof so far that Achillas is planning treachery. And he's an excellent soldier. A pity to throw away a good tool, simply because it may some day prove double-edged."

"Yes, I suppose so," agreed Cleopatra, doubtfully.

In all matters of government, small or large, she relied heavily upon Intef. And rightly so. Intef was shrewd, experienced, and above all completely loyal. He and his daughter Charmion were in fact her only real friends in the wilderness of neutrals and outright enemies through which she had to thread her way.

But he was so terribly cautious, and so unrealistically gentle! He was getting old, to be sure. In any case, maybe by temperament he was better fitted to the temple life than to that of politics?

Not for the first time Cleopatra's thoughts wandered back to the time when her father had been driven from his kingdom, and got it back only by the help of the Roman general. She had been only a young girl at the time, a mere onlooker, taking no active part either for the intrigue or against it.

But she remembered very clearly a certain young cavalry officer who had helped the general, a man called Mark Antony. Now there was a Hercules for you! A man like that would have made short work of the Rat and his kind. What could not a Queen of Egypt do, with a Mark Antony at her side?

An idle dream, of course. There was precious little hope of setting eyes on that handsome young officer again, let alone of enlisting his services. In any case, as her father had found, the services of the Romans were an expensive luxury. The cost of that last occasion still had to be met. On the whole, she thought, the Romans were best kept at a distance from the Two Lands of Egypt.

But this was easier said than done. It was in fact the question of the Romans which brought Cleopatra into the first serious trouble of her reign, three years after it began.

It was well known in Egypt that Rome had recently been in a state of considerable turmoil. At this distance it was hard to understand what it was all about. Other people's politics are always such a puzzle. How, for instance, could any sensible people expect to work such a crazy system as the Romans had, in which two rulers, called "Consuls" were chosen, for one year only, by some complicated system of election in which even the common people had some share? Chopping and changing your rulers every year! How could you expect anything like stability? No wonder the Romans were for ever at each others' throats.

Just now it seemed that the fight was between two generals

(sometimes Consuls as well, sometimes not) called Pompey, and Julius Caesar.

To Egyptian eyes, it looked like six of one and half a dozen of the other. As generals they seemed more or less a match for each other. Pompey had made a name for himself in Asia Minor, which was of course nearly all under the control of the Romans these days, while Julius Caesar had been far away in the West, in the land the Romans named "Gaul".

It was nothing to do with Egypt of course, except that sooner or later one or other of the generals would outwit his opponent. And then it would be as well to be on the winning side. Otherwise the winning general, having mopped up the rest of the world, might turn greedily to Egypt.

But which was to *be* the winning side?

Young Ptolemy, or rather his henchmen, plumped for Caesar. Cleopatra favoured Pompey, partly as being the more legitimate of the two, but mainly because he had once done her father a good turn.

When the Roman generals came finally face to face in Macedonia, and Cleopatra insisted (against Intef's earnest advice) upon sending a squadron of ships to help Pompey, the rift between herself and her brother suddenly gaped wide. It was clear that Achillas and the Palace Guard, and even the bulk of the army, were on the side of young Ptolemy and his followers. But worse, she heard that there were even plots afoot against her life. If she was to keep her share of the kingdom, and her head on her shoulders, she would have to resort to battle, and promptly too.

She fled with a few officers to Syria, to recruit a small army, hoping too that Pompey, in gratitude for her gesture of aid, would perhaps come to her rescue when he had finished with Caesar.

But Pompey was defeated. It had been a shambles, it was said. Thousands of Pompey's men lay dead, while Caesar had lost only a few hundreds. Pompey was in flight, lying low on one of the Greek islands, where his wife and children had already gone.

In Syria Cleopatra heard the news in great dismay. Not only was there now no hope whatever of help from Pompey; by lending even such small aid as she had to the wrong man, she had laid herself open to the enmity of the victorious Caesar.

3 Caesar in Alexandria

TWO MEN stood with their elbows on the bulwarks of a Roman galley, straining their eyes southwards into an empty horizon that danced with heat-haze.

"I always hoped for a chance to see Egypt, Lucius: the Sphinx and all that! But even now this fabled land seems very elusive!" remarked the older one, a man in his fifties. He was lean and muscular, with thin cheeks, a large bony nose, and a head bare of all but a few last strands of grey hair.

"The coast here is so low that you are there almost before you see it, Caesar," replied the other, a man in his forties, so Romanised that there was nothing to betray the fact that he was a Gaul by birth, except perhaps his very blue eyes, and the unhygienic red walrus moustache he obstinately retained.

"Ah, but see!" he added almost at once, "There's your first sight of Alexandria. The famous lighthouse!"

He pointed a little to port of the sun. And there, briefly, stood a ghostly white finger, raised as if in warning.

"The light of it can be seen more than twenty miles away," said Lucius, who had travelled widely before becoming one of Julius Caesar's private secretaries.

Several times in the next hour the white finger broke into the fragments of a mirage, and joined up again. And then, quite suddenly, as Lucius had foretold, they were there, in the great man-made harbour of Alexandria.

As the galley slid in between jagged rocks, they saw before them a great amphitheatre of pale blue water, thick with the gently rocking spars of ships of every nation in the world, from Spain to India.

On the left lay the Lochias peninsula, with its groves of mopheaded palms, the many-coloured lodges of the Royal Palace brilliant against the dark foliage.

On the right towered the three hundred year old "Pharos", tallest and handsomest sea-beacon ever built, nearly four hundred feet of shining white marble, with hundreds of windows, and a spiral plane for the donkeys to climb up, carrying bundles of fuel for the nightly beacon.

"By Hercules, it'd be worth a battle or two to get *that* into Roman hands!" exclaimed Caesar, forgetting in his admiration to tread gently on the national pride of his secretary.

Their approach had evidently been observed, perhaps from that very beacon. For when they tied up at the nearest empty quay, a deputation was already waiting, high-up officials, to judge from their gold chains and collars. These gentlemen seemed to know who he was, even before the *lictors* could step out on to the quay.

"Welcome, Caesar! Welcome to Alexandria!" they chorused, bowing very low, and repeatedly bringing their palms together.

Caesar climbed on to the quay, readjusted the folds of his toga, bent his head slightly, raised his right hand in a dignified Roman salute (he never could bring himself to this oriental kow-towing) and returned their greeting, speaking, like them, in Greek.

"You have some request to make?" he enquired, as the kow-towing continued.

"On the contrary, we come to present to you, Caesar, a token of our goodwill!" they intoned.

Straightening at last, one of them motioned to a nearly naked Nubian soldier, who stepped forward with a spear. On the end of this was stuck a human head, which he thrust forward for Caesar to inspect.

"By all the gods!" exclaimed Caesar.

It was the head of Pompey, some days dead, by the look and smell of it.

"Why in heaven's name have you brought me this thing?" he demanded, with sick disgust.

"But Caesar, this man was your enemy. We bring his head as an assurance of our goodwill and support of your cause!" protested one of the officials, a bloated looking creature with a particularly ornate collar.

"I don't have the honour of your name, sir," said Caesar, looking this fellow over, with instant dislike.

"I am Photinus, Chamberlain to the Pharaoh," announced the man, in a prim tone that said, "Surely you know that?"

"Ah! Well, Photinus, true enough, this *was* my enemy. I had already struck him to his knees, in fair battle. It does me no particular good to see him brought to this. Take the thing *away*, man!" he told the Nubian in sudden uncontrollable disgust, then turned back to the officials.

"Who is responsible for this treachery?" he demanded.

The deputation eyed one another in silent dismay, completely demoralised by this unexpected rejection of their gift, each man wishing the blame on to another.

At last a small, weasel-faced fellow reluctantly spoke up.

"None of us here, Caesar is—er—directly responsible. We understand that a Roman officer who once served with the general Pompey, and perhaps had some personal spite against him, was the man who actually, er, made away with the general. He and a certain Achillas, a very distinguished military gentleman, a Macedonian of course, Commander of the Palace Guard. These two attacked the general with their daggers, three days ago as he landed at Pelusium. It was unfortunate of course that the general's wife and child happened to be looking on from aboard the ship. Very unpleasant indeed. But since the thing had occurred, we felt that Caesar would have been glad to have this, er, visual assurance that his enemy would trouble him no more, and . . ."

"Caesar requires no Egyptian jackals for that or any other

24

assurance!" interrupted Caesar roughly, unable to take any more of this endless rigmarole.

He saw several of the deputation exchange some meaning looks at this.

"But what the Hades, they richly deserve the insult," he told himself. With a contemptuous wave of his hand, he silenced further discussion, and demanded an audience with the King and Queen of Egypt (it was a joint affair here, he understood).

But according to old weasel-face, the Queen was at logger-heads with the King, "the only rightful sovereign", and had gone into Syria to collect a foreign army. The boy-king, with this Achillas, was with the Egyptian army, at the eastern frontier-town of Pelusium, ready to do battle with his sister-wife.

Obviously the Egyptian *civitas* was in a bit of a mess. And where there was a mess it was clear that Rome must step in and clean up. Or so it seemed to Caesar.

Installing himself in the Royal Palace he gave his orders.

First, the body of Pompey must be recovered from the harbour of Pelusium, cremated, and the ashes sent to his widow. The head was to be buried with fitting ceremony in the Grove of Fate.

Second, Ptolemy and Cleopatra were to be summoned to the Palace, for compulsory reunion.

By this time a small fleet of Roman ships, and about 4,000 legionaries, had caught up with Caesar's galley. With these he garrisoned the harbour and the Palace (there were not enough men for the whole city) and settled down to wait for the royal pair.

In the meantime, with Lucius and a token bodyguard of two veteran legionaries, he took a look at Alexandria.

It was a splendid city, there was no doubt of that. Not so old or so elegant as Athens, but everything was on such a grand, spacious scale, with clean, well-paved streets, wide enough for chariots, and about a quarter, or even a third of the city taken up by fine public buildings, theatre and gymnasium, hippodrome and temples, and Court of Justice.

The greatest sights, of course, after the Pharos, were the tomb of Alexander the Great, his original gold sarcophagus now replaced by one of glass, and the famous Royal Library and *Museion,* or Palace of Learning.

There were 700,000 scrolls in that library, the chief librarian told Caesar, on every possible subject from all over the world: scrolls of poetry and prose, on anatomy and the stars, on geometry and the use of levers and wheels, on medicine and on geography.

They were shown, for example, one priceless old map of the world made two hundred years before by the famous geographer, Eratosthenes.

"See! He even knew of the existence of Gaul and the British Isles!" Caesar teasingly pointed out to his Gallic secretary.

They strolled back that morning through the Palace gardens, eating their lunch as they walked, the air sweet with the scent of ripe oranges and citrons and warm fig-leaves, the soft sand of the path trickling agreeably between their sandalled toes.

"I sometimes regret," sighed Caesar, "that I didn't devote my life to philosophy and travel. But there it is. Whether one is to be an Eratosthenes or an Alexander, or a nobody, it's all written in the stars. I have to be content to see the world through the cracks of my life, as it were. . . . Just take this down, Lucius!"

He began to dictate, as they walked, thoughts arising from their morning's sight-seeing, including a note on the tame ibis which had snatched and gobbled up his lunch of bread and onions, yesterday at a crossroads.

These birds, sacred to Thoth, the Egyptian god of wisdom, were everywhere in Alexandria. Fat white creatures with bald heads, they waddled about picking up refuse, and anything good they could snatch.

"Gods, or godlets, of wisdom indeed!" said Caesar, much amused by the incident.

A good master, Lucius was thinking as he scribbled away on the roll of cheap papyrus he carried for such notes. He drove you hard, but was always ready to share a bit of fun, with freeman or slave.

And what a mind, what energy! He couldn't bear to be idle

one minute. Wasn't there enough to see to at the Palace, without putting in all this sight-seeing too?

Screwing enough decent corn for his men out of that crafty old Photinus, for one thing. They were getting some appalling stuff, old and musty enough for the pyramids! And when Caesar complained, the fellow had the impudence to tell him it was quite good enough for folks who lived at other folks' expense.

When Caesar had demanded 10,000,000 of the 17,500,000 drachmas Egypt owed to Rome, he had coolly advised him to go and see to his own affairs, and he should have the money in due course.

The latest petty annoyance was to serve Caesar and his household with wooden and earthen tableware, saying all the gold and silver ware had had to be called in to help to pay this debt. Not that Caesar cared what he ate off so long as it was clean. But the insolence of it was beyond even his tolerance.

He would win in the end. Of that Lucius had no doubt. But he would have to watch his step. It had crossed Lucius' mind several times these last few days that it would not be beyond Photinus and his crew to try to make away with Caesar, just as they might already have done with their king and queen.

However, the next day part at least of this dark suspicion was proved untrue. Ptolemy had arrived at last from Pelusium, and would be pleased to give audience to Caesar, "*post prandium*" as Photinus said with a smirk, showing off one of his few bits of Latin.

Note-taking as usual at this encounter, Lucius was thankful to be able to hide his smiles under his sweeping moustache. Such a pitiful little Pharaoh you never saw, with legs like straws, protruding teeth and a voice see-sawing like a donkey's!

Caesar's judgment was more kindly.

"Poor lad!" he said to Lucius afterwards. "It's a tiresome time of life. Voice breaking, arms and legs shooting out so that your tunic's up to your backside overnight! All the same, if his sister is no different from young Ptolemy, I should have no difficulty in settling this Egyptian affair."

4 *The Carpet Seller*

A FEW days later, just before sunset, Caesar's barber and general factotem, Demades, came to him with a worried expression.

"Sir!" he began, "There is a gentleman—I suppose I should say, with a bundle of carpets to show you."

"Carpets? What should I do with carpets?"

"Quite, sir, but the gentleman won't be told, sir."

"High pressure salesman, eh?" suggested Caesar.

"I don't know what to make of him, sir. The whole thing seems highly suspicious to me. That bundle doesn't seem quite right somehow. If you'll take my advice, which I know you won't, I'd have nothing to do with this carpet salesman, so-called."

"Pooh! You are an old woman, Demades. What harm could a man do with a carpet?" teased his master.

"I may be an old woman. But even I have heard of that wooden horse that brought ruin to Troy. This man's a Greek too, or a Sicilian. It's the same thing."

But Demades had gone about his warning the wrong way. Although at first Caesar had been inclined to refuse to see the carpet man and his wares, his curiosity and pride were aroused, and he could not resist.

"The best way with a Trojan horse is to take the bull by the horns, as they say in Spain," he gaily told Demades. "Bring in this mysterious carpet dealer. Wait a moment, though. Just in case, we'll have a couple of guardsmen in. And get somebody to bring in a lamp or two. I can't inspect carpets properly by twilight!"

But though Caesar spoke jauntily, Lucius noticed that while these preparations were being made, Caesar was unobtrusively laying his sword against the arm of his couch, the hilt within reach.

Presently Demades looked round the door again, his face a comedy-mask of elderly disapproval, and announced:

"Apollodorus, sir! The Sicilian carpet dealer!"

The man came in, bent under his burden, more than seemed really necessary. A roll of carpets may be heavy, but not too heavy for a man of his size, looking more like a gladiator than a salesman. He was trying to carry his bundle with an air of nonchalance, yet his bronzed face, thick neck, and bulging chest muscles were all glossy with sweat. Caesar noticed an odd rigidity about the bundle. And when, coming to a halt a few paces in front of Caesar, he lowered it, and set it down upright, it stood there on end without moving. It was odd.

"Well, Apollodorus," said Caesar, none too genially. "So you have come to pester me with these carpets of yours? I don't need anything like this just now."

"Ah, but wait until you've seen one, Caesar. It is really an extraordinary work of art. The best that Egypt can show. Unique, unrepeatable!"

"My good fellow, one hears this sort of sales-talk every time," retorted Caesar, smiling, but with a watchful eye on both bundle and man.

"But this time it's true, Caesar. Every word of it. I know you will agree when you see what I *may* show you, sir?" he broke off in a sudden earnestness.

"Yes, yes! Open it out and let's have done with it!" rapped out Caesar. "But mind, I make no promise to buy."

"Of course not, sir. No obligation at all, sir."

Apollodorus set about the strings with alacrity. Salesman, gladiator, shipman or porter, whichever he might be, his thick fingers were remarkably deft. In no time at all the last knot

CLEOPATRA

yielded, and with a sweeping, ceremonious gesture he swept off an outer roll, and then a second layer. A third layer dropped heavily to the floor of its own accord.

And there, standing before Caesar, laughing and sneezing, covered with carpet fluff and very dishevelled, was a small, plump, dark-haired young woman.

Caesar's sword clattered to the floor as he sprang to his feet.

"What! Are you a brothel-keeper then, Apollodorus?" he exclaimed, half in laughter, half in vexation at the needless tension of the last few moments.

Apollodorus' face went stiff with horror.

"Sir! Sir!" His voice came out in a hoarse whisper in his consternation at Caesar's reaction. "Can't you see? This is the Queen of Egypt!"

Caesar looked speechlessly at the apparition.

Shaking back her tumbled curls, her black eyes liquid with amusement, her plump cheeks dimpling with laughter, she took a step towards him, and held out one hand, in a regal gesture that said so plainly, "You may kiss it!" that he automatically did so.

"By Jupiter, or Juno, rather! No mistake, this *is* the Queen, sneezes and dust notwithstanding! Every inch of her says so, though there aren't so many inches!" he was thinking as he tasted the carpet fluff on the small warm hand, and struggled to regain his usual composure.

"This is an unexpected pleasure, Queen Cleopatra!" he murmured.

She bestowed a gracious smile to follow the hand.

"You requested my presence, and here I am, as you see," she replied.

He noted with amusement that "requested". He had commanded, not requested the Queen of Egypt's presence. But somehow she was managing to turn obedience into a royal favour!

Then, in a flash, like the twinkling of pigeons' wings against the dark sky, the queen had vanished and there was only a laughing young woman again.

"Oh dear!" she said, covering her face for another delicate sneeze. "I don't know what you must think of me, coming in a c-c-c-*carpet*!"

She gave way to a helpless spasm of laughter at the last word, so infectiously that in a second the whole lot of them were laughing, poker-faced guards included.

"But we couldn't see any other way, could we?" she appealed to the carpet man. Then, to Caesar: "I was at Pelusium when your message came, with enough of an army to fight my way back into Alexandria quite easily. But your message seemed to alter the situation. I don't care for unnecessary bloodshed. I thought it best to slip in quietly, unknown to the enemy. Apollodorus brought me to Alexandria in his own small boat. The difficulty was to get through to you without my brother's knowledge. He's quite capable of having me strangled you know. He's tried it before.

"But now that I'm here under your protection, they will never dare to attempt it. I *am* under your protection, Caesar?" she ended. It was as much a command as a plea.

Caesar hastily pulled himself together.

"You must enlighten me as to the exact situation. And we'll see what can be done," he told her evasively.

"By Jupiter!" he was thinking. "I have to watch this girl! She'll have me for catspaw if I don't look out."

But what a charmer. Not pretty of course, too plump. She would run to fat in later life. But so vivacious, so sparklingly vital, whining and vehement, wheedling and imperious in swift alternation, frank, warm, and above all, intelligent. She reminded him somehow of his daughter Julia, not physically, but in a more elusive way.

Oh, a clever wench all right, worth twenty of that twopenny Ptolemy. It was a thousand pities she had to share the throne with such a creature. A thousand pities too that she was born a woman. The political world was no place for a woman.

A thousand pities, for her own sake. But what fun for the world!

"THIS is delightfully informal!" said Caesar.

It was three days after Cleopatra's carpet debut, and she was giving a state banquet to celebrate the "reconciliation" between herself and Ptolemy, which Caesar had insisted upon as part of the price of his protection.

"Is it so different from a Roman banquet?" she asked, not quite sure whether to take his remark as a compliment.

"Very, and so much pleasanter!" he declared, and not merely out of politeness. He was genuinely enjoying this meal, which seemed to him more of an indoor picnic than a state banquet.

The hall itself was splendid enough with its great pillars topped like lotus flowers. The mosaic floor, representing Alexander the Great at the Battle of Issus, was a marvellous and world-famous work of art. But the actual banquet was casualness itself. Everyone sat where he pleased, the men on low comfortable chairs, all the women except Cleopatra squatting on leather cushions on the floor.

There were no set courses, but a great variety of dishes, all kinds of meat except pork and fish (taboo for royalty it seemed). Everyone took what they fancied, and in any order at all. The food was placed straight into your fingers by female slaves, who seemed to be everywhere, some pretty, some old, but all very deft, moving swiftly about on bare feet, and some practically bare-bodied too, as easy and familiar as your old nurse.

Everybody was decked with flowers. A garland of some pale blue ones had been presented to Caesar at the start of the meal by his hostess. It was already wilting, but still smelt sweet.

"What are these called?" he asked, lifting one flower to sniff at it, and accepting a luscious fig from one of the slaves.

"That is the blue lotus, symbolic of fertility and immortality, our favourite garland for very dear friends," she told him. And something in her eye caused him to colour as he had not done for years. Seeing this, she exclaimed :

"You must be so hot in that toga! Why don't you take it off?"

It was said with such warm concern for his comfort that he had to submit, though in Rome no gentleman would think of discarding his toga in public.

"However, when in Egypt, do as Egypt does!" he remarked.

"Of course!" Cleopatra smiled encouragingly. "You look cooler already. And *so* much handsomer!"

"Oh dear," she thought. "That's a bad slip, implying that there is room for improvement, which heaven knows there is! But perhaps he hasn't noticed. Men often miss such subtleties."

But in case he had, she went on hurriedly :

"I must persuade you sometime to try our Egyptian costume. It would suit you wonderfully well!"

That might or might not be so, Caesar was thinking. But there was no doubt at all that it suited his hostess.

Egypt was famous for its fine linen. In Rome you bought Egyptian if you wanted the best. But could even Egyptian fingers weave cloth so fine, so transparent almost, as the stuff of Cleopatra's robes? No respectable Roman lady would have dared to wear such cloth.

Then there was the make-up. He was used to a good deal of that these days; his own wife used it. But not to this extent.

The Queen of Egypt's face was like a mask : the mask of a cat-goddess perhaps? Great slanting eyes looked out, heavily outlined in black, and twice as large as life. The lids were as green as the jewels in her collar, the eyelashes thick as a camel's.

"But your hair, child? What have you done to your hair?" he suddenly exclaimed.

Twisted into hundreds of tiny black shining ringlets, each with a jewel at the tip, it hung all round her head like a heavy bead curtain, just touching her bare shoulders, and cut in a straight fringe over her eyes. Out of this dark frame the face

33

seemed to be peeping and watching like a little wild animal in a bush.

"You like it?" she said, coquettishly shaking her head. And the ringlets all swung out, and there came to his ears a faint delicious chime, like the sound of rain on a silver dish, and to his nostrils a drift of sweetness from the perfume cone perched on the top of her head.

Then, in the frank, impulsive way he liked so much, she added:

"It's a wig, you know. Traditional Egyptian. I only wear it for state occasions. It's so infernally hot, but very becoming, yes?"

"It is indeed. Perhaps I should wear one myself," agreed Caesar, stroking his own bald head.

"Oh, but baldness is so becoming for a man, it makes him look so clever," was what most women replied to remarks of this kind. Cleopatra did better.

"For myself, I like you just as you are. But if you wanted to do anything about it, I can let you have an infallible recipe, known for hundreds of years to Egyptian women. You take the paws of a dog, one part, kernels of dates, one part, and the hoof of a donkey, one part. Cook it very thoroughly in an earthenware pot, and anoint the head regularly with it, every evening. It really does work, I assure you."

"I'll try it sometime," murmured Caesar, privately resolving that nothing in the world, not even the promise of youthful curls, would bring him to submit to this loathsome concoction.

His hostess, he found, was an excellent listener, the best he had known since his daughter Julia died. She seemed really eager to hear of his campaign in Gaul. Not so much perhaps the military side of it, although even there she showed much interest and a surprisingly unfeminine grasp. What really fascinated her however, was his account of the geography and people of these far-off lands. She had never, herself, been farther North than Syria, or farther West than the edge of the Egyptian border. Ice and snow, for instance, which had so bedevilled one of his later campaigns, were almost beyond her imagination. The idea of a river turning to a sort of glass, strong enough to walk on, or of rain turning into feathers, which accumulated on the ground to the depth of a man's chin, seemed like a fairy story out of Homer.

She was delighted too by his accounts of Britain.

"I have heard of that island, far on the edge of the world. That must have been a strange, dark, dangerous voyage!" she exclaimed with shining eyes.

"On the contrary," said Caesar. "When I was there, in the summer season, the days were longer and the nights shorter than in Rome, or even in Gaul. But it is a miserable land, full of mists and rain, and gloomy with trees."

"And the people?"

"Not entirely despicable as warriors, but like the Gauls, undisciplined."

"Yes, but what are they like as people?"

"Miserable enough. Not quite savages. They know how to make cloth of a kind. They live in huts, squalid, but not entirely comfortless perhaps. They dye their faces and arms with a blue dye, and wear their hair down their backs like women, and on their lips like the Gauls, but they shave their chins. They fight with chariots. And their coastal waters move up and down, some say according to the moon."

"The moon!" marvelled Cleopatra.

She had a trick as she listened of looking straight into his face, with those great eyes of hers, which seemed to imply that he and she were the only people in the world, and he the only one worth listening to. And when something he said especially took her imagination, like this idea of the moon and the British waters, she would wonderingly shake her head, swinging out her hair with that delicious faint rainy sound.

Once or twice, Caesar tried to draw young Ptolemy into the talk. He felt a little sorry for the boy, sitting there beside his sister on the double throne, utterly bored and utterly ignored by her. But the lad was either too sullen or too dull to respond.

At one such attempt Cleopatra broke in contemptuously:

"Oh, never mind him. He doesn't care about geography. He's only interested in vexing me!"

Caesar talked on. There was music; young girls played pipes and harps, and others danced, more nearly naked than he had ever seen. But he was too absorbed in his own talk to pay much attention to either.

But once, when a particularly seductive air caught his ear, he listened for a moment. Like the rest, it was sung in Egyptian, of which he understood not a word.

"It's a love song," Cleopatra told him. "Some day I will translate it for you, yes?"

There was mischief in those great eyes, mischief and something else that set his heart charging off like an undisciplined cavalry unit.

"You fool! Far too old for this sort of thing!" he told himself. But he found it impossible not to respond with a similar message from his own eyes.

"WHAT a pity he's so old!" said Charmion later that night.

It had been their custom, ever since they were girls, to sit together for a little while each night before going to bed, to talk over the day past or the day to come. And since the princess had become a queen, the habit had become the more valued.

Cleopatra reflected a moment. "I must admit," she said, "that when I stepped out of that carpet, I was, for a while, quite bitterly disappointed. 'An old, old man' I thought, 'and ugly too!' Why, even his feet were wrinkled, Charmion, and they weren't very clean either. And I do so hate those togas! Wool is so nasty, unhygienic and smelly! But when you get to know him, you forget his age. His *mind* is so alive, so forward-looking, so inquisitive, and full of fun as well as good sense. Besides, Charmion, he is a very great general, you know. And now Pompey is gone, he has, I suppose, the whole of the Roman legions at his command. If only I could command *him*, Charmion!"

"I wouldn't put it beyond you, my lady!" said Charmion with a laugh.

"You think he's in love with me?"

"I think there's a distinct possibility!"

Cleopatra smiled.

"Frankly, I think so too!" she said. "Old he may be, in years, but tonight he looked at me with the eyes of a boy." She ruminated for several moments, a little glumly, Charmion thought, then roused herself.

"Charmion," she said, her usual self again, "we must cut short our gossip tonight. We must prepare for my Roman Campaign. Will you tell Iras to come and do my hair? This wig is killing me. And tell the chambermaid to change my sheets, I want the best embroidered ones tonight!"

5 *Cleopatra in Love*

CAESAR and Cleopatra, and the indispensable Lucius, were walking in the grounds of the Museion with Sosigenes, one of the resident philosophers, discussing the calendar.

All her life Cleopatra had assumed there were 365 days in a year, twelve months in a year, and thirty days in a month, with five extra feast days; that the year began in the month of Thoth, and that there were three seasons, the season of Flood, the season of the Going out of the Water, and the season of Harvest. All this had seemed to her as natural and immutable as the rising and setting of the sun.

Now she saw clearly enough that all this system was man-made, a time-table for convenience worked out by the brains of men long ago. Nor, according to Sosigenes, one of the best mathematicians in Alexandria, was it even a perfect system, although it was the best so far devised.

"Our year begins, Caesar, on that morning when the star Sirius rises simultaneously with the sun. Now every four years there is a discrepancy here of approximately one day. According to my calculations there is now an error of seventeen days."

"Better than us!" cried Caesar. "We're about three months out at the present time. You see, we have a year of only 355 days. We add an extra month, slap in the middle of Februarius, every two or four years, or whenever anyone has a special political reason to do it."

"It does sound rather a mess," laughed Cleopatra.

"It's chaotic. Some day I intend to clear it all up, and I

believe I couldn't do better than ... Hello!" he broke off. "Who is this coming along? One of your people I think?"

It was Ammonias, a member of Cleopatra's intelligence service, who had come with some shocking news. Photinus, her brother's Chamberlain, had been found an hour since, dead in his bed, apparently strangled.

"Strangled!" exclaimed Caesar, looking hard at Cleopatra, who met his gaze squarely, her face quite expressionless though she had gone rather pale.

"Is anyone particularly under suspicion?" he asked, since for the moment Cleopatra seemed either disinclined or unable to question her man.

Ammonias shook his head.

"Not a clue!" he said. "Only the marks of the fingers on his neck, which are clearly those of a man. We shall make a thorough investigation of course, but—" he shrugged his shoulders, and turned to address Cleopatra, putting Caesar into his place as interloper in this purely domestic business.

"There is another piece of news, my lady, which may or may not have some bearing on this crime. Your sister Arsinoe has disappeared. Her bed had not been used. She must have slipped away early in the night. And, my lady—"

"Yes?"

"Commander Achillas also has gone, it is thought to Pelusium. Whether or not with your sister is not known."

"Of *course* they've gone off together!" cried Cleopatra excitedly. "Why, they've been thick as thieves this last six months. Everybody knows that! Thank you, Ammonias!' she broke off, suddenly recovering her authority. "I shall—my brother and I will of course insist upon a complete investigation into this murder. Come to me later at the Palace, and we will decide what must be done."

The man was barely out of earshot when, turning to Caesar, she exclaimed:

"I had to say that of course. But frankly I don't care who committed this crime. He's done us a good turn. We were none of us safe with Photinus around! I assure you, Caesar, it's a miracle that you were not the one found with marks about your neck! That's what they've been plotting, as I've tried to warn you." She shivered, rather theatrically, it seemed to Caesar, yet with real tears in her eyes.

"Yes, I'm glad they got the wretch!" she repeated, with a cold ferocity so open that he could not, somehow, be as shocked as he felt he ought. "That's one enemy the less. And as for Achillas and my crocodile sister, I thought something was brewing, and I'm glad it's out in the open at last. Now we know where we are."

"Oh, we do?" said Caesar.

He was chilled by this murder, she could see, and clearly had more than a slight suspicion that the deed was hers, or at least done by her command.

Well, let him suspect. She was not going to defend herself, unless directly accused. She had no idea who had done it, although there were plenty among her servants, good loyal creatures, capable, she knew, of doing much more for her sake. For that matter, how did Caesar know it was not one of his own loyal and faithful servants—Demades, for instance, his devoted barber-valet?

Two days later came fresh news from Pelusium. Arsinoe and Achillas were there with the Egyptian army, preparing to march upon Alexandria.

"You see?" said Cleopatra.

"Yes, as you remarked the other day, now we know where we are," replied Caesar. His look and tone were somewhat grim, yet also she felt, elated.

"He'll fight for me all right. He can't resist this challenge!" she told herself.

"What a couple of idiots," she said to Caesar, "They can't possibly win."

"Don't underrate your Achillas, he's Roman-trained. And don't overrate my own powers. I've barely 4,000 men with me at present. This may be a hard struggle. We shall do our best for you, but the outcome is with the gods, as always. Meanwhile," his face now was quite grim, devoid of any elation whatever, "no more strangling, my girl, if you please."

"There has been none by my orders! And there is no need, now I have your help!" she said with dignity.

That "my girl" did not offend her. She knew that it was only his way of expressing his affection for her, which was growing day by day. And in his affection lay her only hope, at present her only power.

Alexandria, as Caesar saw clearly enough during those first days of sight-seeing, was easy to capture, but very hard to defend. For much of that winter, the inadequate Roman forces were more or less besieged in the Palace. At one time even the water supply was cut off by the enemy, who blocked the aqueducts which supplied the royal quarter of the city, and even pumped up sea-water, with special engines, into the Palace reservoirs.

Caesar was not going to be beaten that way. Roman soldiers were used to digging and ditching during their campaigns. He set his men to work in the Palace gardens to dig new wells, and in one night they had tapped enough water for the whole of the beleaguered community.

Fairly soon in the struggle two events worked in favour of Caesar and Cleopatra. First, Arsinoe, not even consistent in her treachery, had Achillas murdered, promoting her chamberlain, Ganymede, into his place. "The Crocodile's a fool, he never was any judge of men!" commented Cleopatra.

Secondly, an extra legion arrived to reinforce Caesar's extremely meagre force. They had some difficulty in landing. Ganymede might not be quite as clever as his predecessor, but he was no fool. Under his command the Egyptian navy harried the Roman ships, both inside and outside the harbour. At one point the Roman ships in the harbour were in such danger of falling into Egyptian hands that Caesar landed the crews and ordered some of the vessels to be set on fire.

Unfortunately the flames spread to the nearby Museion, and

the Library was almost burnt down. By the frantic efforts of the chief librarian and his staff, most of the books were saved, but 40,000 irreplaceable scrolls were destroyed.

Caesar greatly regretted this catastrophe.

"But after all," he consoled the librarian, who was shattered by the loss, "it's the minds of men that matter, not their products. Other scholars will be born to write other great books."

"But not *these* books, Caesar!" wailed the librarian.

"We shall replace them!" said Cleopatra grandly. "There must be copies of at least some of these scrolls. We shall send everywhere, and replace them when this war is over!"

Caesar smiled, half flattered, half amused by her air of complete confidence in him.

He was far from sharing it himself. For weeks, well into the New Year (Roman Calendar) neither side seemed able to win a decisive advantage. At one point, in a desperate effort to shift the balance, he attacked the rocky island of Pharos, and the breakwater joining it to the mainland. The only result was partly to destroy the breakwater. At one time he really thought his men were going to be beaten outright.

He was directing from the breakwater at the time, and seeing the ships so hard-pressed, jumped into a small skiff to go to their assistance. Spotting him immediately, several Egyptian vessels bore down upon the tiny cockle-shell, with its one oarsman. Caesar had to dive in and swim for his life.

Fortunately he was a strong swimmer, and even in winter the water here was not cold. But hampered by his armour and by the fact that he had some important letters in his hand which he had to hold up with one hand to keep dry, he only just made it to the Roman galley, and lost a very good cloak too.

Cleopatra had never admired her elderly lover more than on that day.

"He's a fighter, and no mistake! Small wonder his men adore him!" she said, and never had the slightest doubt that he would win in the end.

In the spring the tide turned. Mithridates, King of Pergamum in Asia, a friend both to Cleopatra and to Caesar, had been busy during the winter recruiting an army in Syria. Now he marched upon Pelusium, took it, and came on half-way across the delta of the Nile.

Ganymede, joined months ago by Ptolemy and his supporters, had to withdraw his forces from Alexandria, and march east to meet the invader.

"Now they're done for! We can attack them easily from the rear!" exulted Cleopatra when the news reached her.

"It's a possibility," admitted Caesar, showing the superstitious caution of a veteran campaigner. He had learned long since to take nothing for granted. In fact, victory was now almost a foregone conclusion. The Egyptian troops, caught between Caesar's and those of Mithridates, never had much chance. Great numbers of them were slaughtered, and Ganymede and Arsinoe were taken prisoners.

Amongst the dead was young Ptolemy.

6 A Nile Journey

IN the late spring, peace and order was restored. Now that Cleopatra was established as the only lawful ruler of Egypt, she decided to journey up the Nile to show herself to as many of her people as possible, and confirm their loyalty.

Julius Caesar went with her. There was much to be done in Rome, and also in the Roman Provinces of Africa and Asia. But must a man's whole life be spent in warfare? And might there not be knowledge of great future value to himself and to Rome to be gained by such a journey? So Julius Caesar persuaded himself. The truth was that he could not resist the charm of Cleopatra's company, plus the opportunity to satisfy a long cherished desire, to see the Egyptian antiquities.

It was like a journey in a dream. Day after day, mile after mile, as they lay in the shade of the richly tasselled awnings, lulled by the rhythmical creak and splash of thirty pairs of oars, the land of Egypt seemed to glide past. It was the same scene, over and over again: fields of ripe corn, or green clover, or scented bean-flowers; tufted clumps of date-palm, with their knots of orange or brown fruit; low ramparts of stony mountains, scored deep with vertical clefts like marks of suffering, white in the midday glare, pink and gold in the sunset. There was a strange magic in the very monotony of it that released the heart from the fretfulness of ambitions and anxieties, soothed the spirit, enchanted the mind.

The royal barges were not the only travellers on this brown, thousand-mile water highway. They met or passed or were followed by dozens of other craft, small and large, some working up-river with one great sail like a swan's wing, swollen in the northern breeze, others drifting oar-less and sail-less down the current, at two or three miles an hour, laden with pink water jars, or mounds of striped melons, or great cubical stacks of golden straw.

A small flock of white herons sometimes flapped slowly by, low over the water, or kingfishers flashed through the reeds like blue needles. Someone would point out a pelican, gulping a fish into the great bag it carried under its beak, like a gladiator's net.

It was Pachon, the second month of the Season of Harvest. In the fields the brown reapers sang as they bent over their sickles. In one place the oxen already trod the threshing-circle, while the driver sang, over and over again, a song which Cleopatra translated for Caesar:

> Get along oxen,
> Thrash the corn faster,
> The straw for yourselves
> The corn for your master!

The land of the Nile was full of singing. Ferrymen in their papyrus-bundle boats sang as they paddled to and fro. Palanquin bearers sang to assure Cleopatra that she made the palanquin lighter than when empty. The man at the prow sang out the depths as he prodded the water with his long pole, feeling for the treacherous, shifting sandbanks of the Nile.

On moonlit nights the royal procession sometimes went on all night for the sake of the coolness. Then Charmion would sing to them some ancient love song. Or she would tell them Egyptian stories. She knew one about a "doomed" prince, who having escaped the Dog, the Serpent, and the Crocodile, married a princess who lived in a tower with seventy windows. She told another about a shipwrecked sailor, befriended on an island by a kindly she-serpent, who sent him home with a cargo of myrrh, eye-paint, incense, ivory, greyhounds and giraffes' tails. And there was one rather horrifying one about a rich and wicked man who ended in the Underworld with a door working on a pivot in his right eye, while the poor man he had robbed enjoyed all the rich man's funeral gear.

If there was no moon, they pulled in and moored for the night. It was so warm that it was possible to sleep on deck, wrapped only in a sheet. Lying there, under a sky spread thick with the stars of Africa, the boat softly wapping the water as it swung on its mooring-rope, the warm body of his little Egyptian queen in his arms, Caesar was aware as never before in his busy life, of the strangeness and the grandeur and the mystery of the world.

"What are the stars, I wonder!" he said on one such night.

She turned in his arms to look up with him.

"Some say they are the souls of great or sinless people—but how can we know?" she replied.

"I once heard a philosopher," went on Caesar, "who believed that behind the sky is a great globe of fire, of which we see only these points, where the fabric is pierced."

Cleopatra frowned, and then smiled. He could feel the double movement of her skin against his cheek.

"Like a charcoal brazier. How terribly prosaic!" she protested. "Now there is an old Egyptian story that the sky is a goddess called Nut. She bends backwards like an acrobat over the earth, her hands at the west, her feet at the east, her back spangled with stars. She was one of the four children of the sun. My father had a picture of her painted on the roof of his temple at Dendyra. You shall see it by and by. I think that's a much prettier idea than your charcoal brazier!"

Not all their days were spent aboard the royal barge. At each important city or temple the party landed, and there were ceremonies to be gone through, more and more tedious as the tour proceeded and the heat increased, but unavoidable. As a half-god Cleopatra was welcomed, and as a half-god she was expected to endure. And Caesar too found he was expected to participate to some extent in these rituals. But he was able also

46

to put in quite a quantity of the sight-seeing he had hoped for.

The pyramids, naturally, ranked high in his list of priorities. He was surprised to learn, however, that there were about a score of these ancient monuments, scattered along the west side of the Nile valley for nearly a hundred miles. It would be impossible to visit them all.

"And many of them, I am told, are mere heaps of broken stones," Cleopatra told him.

"Then let us see the best ones only," he agreed.

After the ceremonies at Heliopolis, therefore, they tied up at the island of Roda where Caesar wanted to see the Nilometer, a simple but ingenious instrument for measuring the height of the Nile floods. From here they set out before dawn with a minimum of attendants, riding on a couple of strong Egyptian donkeys, dirty white in colour.

It was a six or seven mile ride. They were only half way there when the sun rose, with its usual rapidity in Egypt, like a great rosy ball bobbing up out of water. And there, behind the slender columns of a grove of palms, stood those amazing monuments, enormous even three miles away, their stumpy points coloured a delicate pink by the sunrise, the lower halves standing in a thin bluish veil of morning mist.

By the time they dismounted at the pyramid of Cephron, every scrap of mist had vanished. The sun burned their backs like a branding iron. The dry sand roasted their feet. The stony sides of the pyramid gave out currents of hot air like the walls of an oven.

They huddled into a small shadow cast by the broken portico of a temple nestling like a calf against the great flank of the pyramid, and breakfasted on a few dates, a loaf, and a jar of wine, well content with the expedition, yet secretly a little disappointed with the pyramids themselves, now they were face to face with them.

However, they had no reservations as to the Sphinx, the

strange beast with a lion's body and a man's head, cut out of the living, lion-coloured rock.

"They say there is a temple buried in the sand between its paws," said Cleopatra.

They were standing at the base of one of the paws, which must have been over fifty paces long, looking up into that huge enigmatic face of stone, with its wind-chapped lips and its deep, weather-scoured eyesockets. "A god, or a Pharaoh?" marvelled Caesar.

"It is the same thing," Cleopatra reminded him. "But nobody knows which Pharaoh. It is so very old."

Memphis, their next stopping place, was one of the oldest cities in Egypt, with temples to a bewildering variety of gods, some still in the state of ruin to which the Persians had reduced them, but many partly restored and swarming with priests and their hangers-on.

Besides the chief temple to the god Ptah, where Cleopatra and her dead brother had been crowned, there were temples to the mother-goddess Hathor, and to the lion-goddess Sekhmet, a shrine for Anubis, the dog-god of the underworld (being used at present as a sort of headquarters for the desert police) and another for the goddess Astarte, worshipped by the many foreigners of this city.

Connected with Astarte's temple were a number of shrines to a fat and ugly little dwarf-god called "Bes", to whom Cleopatra, very much to Caesar's surprise, seemed to pay special attention.

"He is the protector of women, you see, particularly in childbirth," she explained in a manner which puzzled him to decide if she were in earnest or not.

What puzzled him even more was the number of sacred animals in this country: dogs and cats, lions and bulls, cows, crocodiles and even fish. How could an intelligent human being bring himself to believe in such a menagerie of gods?

This sacred black bull, Apis, for instance: just south of the temple of Ptah stood his shrine, his luxurious stall, and the great rambling catacombs where the mummified remains of his ancestors were interred.

"I hope the present Apis doesn't die just yet," said Cleopatra, as they inspected the vast embalming hall, with its bull-sized alabaster slabs and basins. "It costs a fortune to bury one. But it's one of the inescapable duties of a Pharaoh. My father had to pay out a hundred talents, and that was only for the white cow, the mother of Apis."

But the visit which amazed and amused Caesar most of all was the one they made to the temple of the god Suchos, in the city the Greeks called "Crocodilopolis".

After a ceremonial meal at the temple, the party went out to the sacred lake in which the god was kept, the officiating priest carrying with him from the royal table a cake, some pieces of roast meat, and a pitcher of wine mixed with honey.

The sacred creature lay basking in the sun on the baked mud at the water's edge. Its great snout hung half-open, its horny eyelids reduced to evil slits.

As the party approached it widened the slits a fraction, but made no other movement. Nor did it offer the slightest resistance when two of the priests went and seized its jaws, opened them wide like a pair of nutcrackers, put the cake in between the rows of nail-like teeth, then the meat, and finally poured the wine down its throat. All this it suffered meekly enough. Then suddenly it clapped-to its jaws, swished sideways into the water, and swam across to the far side at a speed amazing in so sluggish-looking a monster.

Just as the royal party turned to go, another party of visitors arrived with offerings. Immediately, the two priests took the gifts, dashed round the lake, seized the monster as he emerged, and forcibly fed him for the second time.

"Well worshipped, good priests!" shouted Caesar, unable to contain his amusement at this ludicrous sight. Fortunately the priests were out of hearing, and after a moment's hesitation, Cleopatra joined in his laughter—very heartily too.

49

"But seriously," he protested as they strolled back to the temple. "Do you believe this creature to be a god?"

"Not exactly, not in himself. Simply a manifestation—as it were—a materialisation, of one of the gods. Not, I must confess," she admitted with a droll grimace, "one of my favourite deities!"

It was well into the month of Pachon now (April by the Roman calendar). With every day and with every mile upstream the heat became more intolerable. Caesar, who had long since abandoned his toga, was obliged to shed his woollen tunic also, and went clad like a native in no more than a loin-cloth.

"Anybody but you would have abandoned the sight-seeing before now!" Cleopatra told him. She was suffering badly from the heat herself. Even her spirits began to wilt at the thought of all the temples yet to come. But Caesar, rather conscious of his fifty-four years, and determined to prove he was still in his prime, refused to give in.

"It's not so long since I conquered Gaul. I'm not going to be beaten by the Egyptian sun-god," he declared.

So they saw the City of Dogs, and the City of Thoth with its cemetery of mummified baboons. They saw the famous Colossi of Memnon, one of whose legs was supposed to give forth a singing note at sunrise. It failed to perform for Caesar.

They toiled in the blazing sun up into the barren mountains west of Thebes to see the Tombs of the Kings, which were like great honeycombs in the bare rocks, all empty, plundered of their contents many centuries ago, but wonderfully painted with red, yellow and blue pictures of life in ancient times.

They plodded along the avenue of sphinxes, lapped to the paws or the chins in blown sand, to the mighty temple of Amon-Rè at Karnak. This was the most imposing temple of all, with its pylons and tall fat pillars, and its even taller obelisks of shining pink granite, glittering high above the tops of the palm trees.

Amongst a maze of smaller sanctuaries at Karnak was one

built by a member of Cleopatra's own family, in honour of the hippopotamus goddess, Tuart, protector of pregnant women.

It was here that Cleopatra confided to Caesar something he had been suspecting for several weeks now. She was carrying a child, Caesar's child.

CAESAR'S instinctive reaction was one of pure joy. They were in public, at the head of a procession of dignitaries, or he would have embraced her immediately. Instead he took her hand and pressed it, in a surge of tenderness and gratitude.

"The best news for many a year!" he exclaimed. "I have no children as you know. I did have one daughter, by my first wife. But she died when I was in Gaul." In childbirth, he had been about to add, but held it back out of consideration for Cleopatra.

He was silent for a while, but she saw his face relax into a pleased smile. Presently he went on:

"A child! So the old man isn't incapable after all. It must have been the women who were at fault! My second and third marriages were only political. Where there is no natural inclination, fertility perhaps is less."

"There was certainly plenty of 'natural inclination' in our marriage!" laughed Cleopatra, gratified by this reception of her news.

"Our marriage?" repeated Caesar, stopping for a moment and eyeing her sharply. "Ah well—we may put it like that, perhaps, for decency's sake. Yes—call it a marriage by all means!" he conceded, as he moved on again, with a grin that by now had seriously alarmed her.

"What do you mean, 'call' it a marriage, Caesar?" she retorted haughtily. "You are my husband, and the father of this child."

"Ah yes, in the eyes of this hippopotamus goddess, no doubt," he mocked.

The royal party had reached the outer pylon of the temple now. Cleopatra stopped and imperiously signalled all to go on ahead.

"Come into the shade," she said to Caesar, drawing back into a small triangle of black in the angle of the massive stone gateway. The shadow of one of the four pennants on its top fluttered across her face, which had turned very pale. She panted visibly from the heat, which her burdened body had found much harder to bear these last ten days.

"Caesar," she began again, "I took it for granted that you realised that, in the eyes of all my people and myself, you are indeed my husband."

"I'm not aware of having undergone any ceremony to that effect."

Her eyes blazed with fury at that, and the sweat burst out in a hundred bright points on her face.

"In Egypt we have no need of ceremonies!" she flung at him. "If a man and a woman live together, in love and in earnest, as we have done, that *is* a marriage. Of course, if there is property there may be an agreement later drawn up on papyrus. But this is not necessary unless they wish. I never thought it necessary between you and me. You know that all I have is yours. And the help you gave to me last winter—that I thought was given freely! But if you wish to dissolve the marriage, you are free to do so. You have lived with me for more than five months. That is all our Egyptian law requires."

He looked at her, aghast, but convinced now of the truth of her statement.

"Cleopatra," he said at last. "I assure you this is news to me."

"But all those ceremonies in the temples—why did you think you were there at my side, if not as my husband?"

He looked embarrassed.

"I'm afraid I assumed I was a sort of male . . . concubine! Oh, I didn't object." His voice and expression warmed for a moment. "Joking apart, Cleopatra, this has been a time of great happiness to me. You have, truly, been as dear to me as my wife. But the fact remains," his face was hardened again, "according to Roman law, you are *not* my wife."

"Then make me so!"

"My dear girl, I have already one Roman wife."

"Then divorce her."

They looked steadily at each other; in the silence their two wills clashed in the air like bright swords.

"I should need to think hard about that," he said at length. And that was all that he could be brought to say, either then or later.

Not that she attempted again to tackle him directly on the question of their marriage. It had been a bad mistake, she realised, to allow herself so open a challenge. For the rest of their journey she set herself to work upon him indirectly, to restore the magical thread which had drawn him to her feet in the first place.

Never in the six months that Caesar had known her, was Cleopatra more bewitching than now. She was everything by turns: queen or coaxing girl, witty as Minerva or voluptuous as Aphrodite, humble pupil or imperious mistress.

Do what she would, she felt that something had changed between them. He loved her still, she felt certain. He was if anything kinder and more gentle than before. She never tried to tie him to her company except for the necessary public appearances. But he still seemed to seek her out of his own free will. His delight in the thought of the coming child continued. Yet there was no doubt about it. The journey downstream was not the idyll that the journey upstream had been.

Ah well, perhaps when the child was born, and especially if it were a boy, he might think differently about this question of marriage? Yes, if only she could keep Caesar in Egypt until then, all might yet be well.

But when they got back to Alexandria there were letters waiting for Caesar from Rome, with details of events which required his urgent attention in Asia Minor; Capadocia and

Armenia had been overrun and the Roman province of Pontus was occupied by a rebel son of Mithridates.

"Impossible. I've stayed too long already," declared Caesar when Cleopatra begged him outright to stay at least until his child was born. "What could I do if I stayed? I can't bear the child for you. That's your business!" he told her, as brutal as she had ever known him.

"That's so." She accepted this defeat, with her usual realism. "But when you have put things in order in Asia, will you come back?"

He hesitated. She watched his face, hardening and softening and finally hardening against her.

"No, my dear girl. After that, I'm afraid Rome will need my attention."

"But Egypt needs you too! Think of it, this ancient, splendid country. It's crying out for a king, and you—you are so clearly a man in need of a kingdom!"

She thought for a moment she had got him with that. But he slipped away once more.

"No, no. Not for me, Cleopatra. I'm no king. Just a battered old Roman general. Rome, I know, is little more than a poor British village, compared to Alexandria. But it's where I belong. That's where my work lies."

"But what shall I do without you!" she almost wailed.

"You'll do very well. You should marry that younger brother of yours. Isn't that what your friend Intef has been urging? Yes, I know!" he interrupted her exclamation of disgust. "He's only eleven. No earthly good either as man or king. But that's just the point. You'd be sole ruler, in effect. And Rome will keep her distance, I promise you that: in the background in case of more trouble, which I don't anticipate. You're well established now. Quite capable of carrying on alone. And who knows, Cleopatra, perhaps our child will be a son? Bring him up well. And when he comes to manhood, Egypt may enter a new golden age. Or even before that. There have been great queens before now, one or two!"

Three weeks later he sailed with most of his men, leaving behind a small garrison under a competent Roman commander.

"Come to Rome sometime!" he called to her as his galley slid slowly from the quay.

About six weeks after he had gone, in the month of Thoth, the child was born. It was a boy, small but lively, and as bald as a coot, the image of his father, as all the court ladies, from Charmion downward, were agreed. He was named Ptolemy Philopater Philometer Caesar. But from the very beginning everyone called him "Caesarion", that is "Little Caesar".

7 *The Ides of March*

THE FOLLOWING summer, hearing that Caesar had won his campaigns in Pontus and North Africa, and gone home, Cleopatra invited herself and her one-year-old boy to Rome, in a manner impossible for Caesar to refuse.

Not that his welcome was in the least cold or even reluctant. There was an impressive reception of officials to meet her ship at the port of Rome. And in Rome itself she found that he had made over to her his own house on the Janiculum hill on the right bank of the Tiber, where some of the wealthiest Romans had villas with the gardens which had recently become so fashionable.

Of course, it was all on a miniature scale compared to her own property in Alexandria. But she rather liked that.

"It's like living in a doll's house," she told Charmion.

The morning after her arrival, Caesar himself came to see that all was comfortable.

"I'm sadly changed, I know," she remarked, after the first greetings and enquiries were over, rather shocked for her part to see how much balder and more haggard he looked than she had remembered.

"Not in the least, or if at all, only for the better," he assured her, though secretly he thought, 'Heavens, how fat she's getting. Why, she's no beauty after all.'

But he had not been in her company for five minutes before he was once more under the old Cleopatra-spell. She was so delightfully alive, so interested in everything he showed her and so eager to see and hear more. And such fun.

On the Capitoline Hill, for instance, she fairly burst out laughing at the sight of the statue of the wolf—the sacred wolf, suckling the sacred twins, Romulus and Remus, founders of Rome itself.

"So! In Egypt we have our crocodile god. In Rome you have your wolf!" she teased him.

"Well no, not exactly a god!" protested Caesar. "More a sort of semi-sacred creature. And there are in fact many who question the whole myth, particularly as we do not know whether by the word *lupa* our forefathers intended 'a female wolf' or 'a prostitute'!"

Cleopatra laughed.

"We too have many puzzling myths like that," she said, mischievously.

"What a piffling city, Charmion!" Cleopatra remarked after that first day's sight of Rome. "Interesting of course, but *so* provincial. Those old bridges over the Tiber, clever enough I suppose as an engineering feat. But after all, the Tiber's little more than a gutter you know, compared to the Nile. I can't imagine the Romans will ever bridge that!"

"I should think not indeed!" agreed Charmion indignantly.

"Their roads are first rate of course," admitted Cleopatra. "And the water system is good, though no better than we have in Alexandria. But the public buildings are mere hovels. Take that little Temple of Vesta, quite pretty, but very insignificant. As for the Regia, where the kings in olden days used to live, why, a provincial Egyptian tax-gatherer would turn his nose up at that! And the streets, Charmion, they're so narrow and filthy. The best are no better than our Alexandrian slums."

"As for their women," suggested Charmion.

"Oh, the women! Bundled up in their woolly *stolas*, as they call them, like a lot of fat old sheep!" She giggled.

"Any minute you think they'll go 'ba-a-a' in your face!" said

Charmion, pacing the room and mimicking a Roman matron, and throwing them both into fits of helpless laughter.

"Oh, Charmion! I don't know how I could endure Rome if I hadn't got you to laugh with!" said Cleopatra.

It was lucky that Caesar had not asked for her first impressions, or apologised for the shortcomings of his native city except for the weather which had been unpleasantly sweaty.

"Even a Dictator can't do anything about that!" he had joked.

There was little else that he could not do, it seemed to Cleopatra.

King, of course, as he had so often explained to her, was a dirty word to the Romans. So instead they called him *Imperator* and *Dictator*. She thought it came to much the same thing. And why not indeed? The general of the legions which had now mastered the whole world, or all of it that counted, had surely the right to be master in Rome itself?

If he needed money he simply sent his servants off to the Treasury. He alone appointed officers of the army. He alone could declare war or peace. He alone tried cases of treason, either in public at the Forum or in his own house. He had first place in the Senate, the Roman council of Elders. He was in control of the elections, nominating which families were to be promoted to the nobility and recruited to a place in the Senate. He had raised its numbers to nine hundred, half at least of which were "his" men.

It seemed the Senate could not honour him too much. They had voted him the right to wear in public a purple toga and a crown of laurel leaves, and to sit in the Forum on a golden chair. Could a man get nearer to kingship than that?

As for the common people, he was almost their god.

On the success of a military adventure, a Roman general was entitled to celebrate with a "triumph", a grand procession of dancers and flute players, and images of the gods, and prisoners of war in chains, along the Sacred Way to the Capitol for

sacrifices, and back to the Circus Maximus for games and entertainment.

Caesar was due for no less than four such celebrations, one
for the Gallic war, one for victory in Pontus, a third for Egypt,
and a fourth for the latest victory in Africa over the sons and
followers of the late Pompey.

Cleopatra was one of the privileged spectators at the last
two: splendidly staged affairs, with a procession of elephants
from Africa, carrying lighted torches in their trunks.

Among the captives from Egypt walked Cleopatra's sister
Arsinoe. It was good of course to se her old enemy the Crocodile safely in chains. But what if Caesar had happened to take
the other side in that quarrel?

"*I* should have been walking there, and she up here!" said
Cleopatra to herself, a shiver passing over her skin at the
thought. "But no!" she corrected herself in fierce contempt.
"They'd never have got me walking there in shame! I would
have killed myself first!"

Caesar was lavish. As well as the formal processions, there
were chariot races and gladiatorial displays galore for the
people, as well as the 100 *denarii* he distributed to every citizen,
and the cash bounties for the troops.

Cleopatra found chariot races a bore, and the gladiators disgusting. In which Caesar more or less agreed.

"It's no pleasure to me I assure you to see a man die. I often
get on with my correspondence during these wretched affairs.
But that doesn't make for popularity!"

"The masses simply can't understand how much work falls to
their rulers," said Cleopatra, with the quick sympathy of one
who knew. The pressure of work upon Caesar was indeed tre-
mendous, enough to kill a lesser man. After fifty years or more
of civil war, Rome was in a state of social and economic chaos,
and his were the only hands strong enough to restore some sort
of order. Everything, it seemed, had to pass through them.

As if the day to day running of the state were not enough, he
had all kinds of plans in his head for the future, only one of

which he had time and energy just then to put into operation. With the help of Sosigenes, who had come out with Cleopatra's retinue, the Roman calendar was at last put on the sensible Egyptian footing (not without a good deal of resistance from certain conservative senators, who complained that Caesar was now aiming even at the control of the stars).

Cleopatra was seeing less and less of Caesar. He could seldom spare time until late in the evening, and he never once stayed overnight. This she accepted. He had, after all, a wife in Rome. In a little place like this the tongue of scandal was so easily set wagging. She never reproached him, nor even attempted to coax him to her bed. It was not for love that she had come to Rome, but for the sake of her son and for Egypt.

Caesar's attitude to their son was ambiguous, to say the least.

The first time, the very first time they had set eyes on each other, the child had lifted up his chubby arms and crowed with delight.

"See, he knows you, he's usually so shy with strangers. He knows his father!" cried Cleopatra in pleased surprise.

But Caesar had not appeared to share her pleasure.

"Nonsense, sheer superstition," he had scoffed, quite rudely. "Most children take to me : I don't know why," almost as if he wanted to disown his fatherhood. He was obviously fond of the child, and Caesarion certainly adored his father. But she noted that he was always referred to as "your son", never "our son", still less "my son". And once, when she commented on the boy's likeness to himself, he positively winced.

"I see a faint resemblance to you," said Caesar, "but he might as well be Ptolemy's son for all the likeness to me."

"How can you say so?" cried Cleopatra indignantly. "You know he's your son. You know very well that the Rat was never allowed in my room from the first day I met you. And he never shared my bed. I made him sleep on the floor right from the start."

"All right, all right! I never said he was not my son. Only

that I could see no likeness. Babies never *are* like anybody but themselves," Caesar soothed her.

Clearly the time was not yet ripe to put forward the proposal she had come on purpose to make : that he should publicly acknowledge Caesarion as his son and heir in Roman law, as well as her heir by Egyptian law.

It puzzled her why he should balk at this. To herself he showed every sign of continued affection, and not only in private. Publicly too he had honoured her by placing a statue of her in the temple of Venus. Now the Julian family claimed descent from Venus, as she knew, so that this statue was as much as to say : "Cleopatra is a member of the family of Julius Caesar". His act had greatly offended certain members of the Roman aristocracy, to whom it was almost a blasphemy. But his power was now so great that he had almost ceased to pay attention to such feelings. Why then not take this final step of recognition?

She had intended to stay a few months. But November came and still she had not achieved her purpose. And now Caesar had once more to leave Rome. The sons of Pompey, defeated in North Africa, had escaped to Spain and there built up a powerful force of thirteen legions, about 78,000 men. Caesar's presence was necessary to subdue them again. There was every likelihood of its being a brief campaign, he told Cleopatra. According to the latest news from Intef, left at home in charge of her affairs in Egypt, all was well there. She made up her mind to stay for a few months longer in the hope of succeeding in her object when Caesar returned.

IT was bitterly cold in Rome that winter : miserably, damply cold, with a grey, heavy sky for days on end. Once there was even a fall of the strange thing Caesar had told her about, called snow : pretty enough in the air, but clammy and ugly on the ground.

Now for the first time Cleopatra understood the value of those horrible woolly objects which the Romans put on their feet, smelly, unhygienic things called socks. Before very long she had to send a slave out across the Tiber bridge to buy a pair to keep her feet warm, at least in private. Not even a Roman winter was going to make her deform her pretty feet with these objects in public. She was determined on that point. But sandals were impossible. This Roman cold turned one's feet such an unbecoming blue. She had to get herself a pair of red leather boots for outdoor wear, and a pair of warm felt slippers for indoors.

She discovered also that the Roman women's stolas were really very sensible even about the house, and absolutely essential out in the streets.

Her household had to be similarly equipped, and an extra supply of charcoal for the braziers brought in. Life was not endurable without at least one brazier per room. It was all very expensive, but it would have been uneconomic to oblige even the slaves to live as at home, half-naked and without artificial warmth. They would all have died of cold, and she would only have to buy a new household, probably at extortionate Roman prices.

"If only I'd known, Charmion," Cleopatra frequently lamented, "I doubt if I'd have stayed!"

It was lonely and boring now Caesar was away, as well as so miserably cold. To a certain extent he had forced her entry into some of the patrician families. But now, in his absence, she was more or less ignored.

"You know, Charmion, I haven't really a single friend in this place apart from Caesar himself. I don't know what I'd do without you and my little boy."

But she was here. And seeing she was here, she was determined the time should not be wasted.

In a very short time she had agents planted all over the city in strategic places such as the wine shops or the barbers: a spider's web in the centre of which she sat hidden, gathering a mass of disconnected information, political, social or pure scandal.

She even indulged in a little personal spying. Attended by a male slave in Roman dress, she and Charmion, bundled up like a pair of old sheep in their voluminous stolas, would now and then go prowling about the crowded streets up the Aventine Hill, or mingle with the bustling throng in the Forum. Stolas were a wonderful disguise they found, easily looped across one cheek in moments of danger. Not that this often proved necessary. Rome was full of people from all over the world, many of whom had adopted Roman dress. There was nothing about these two to attract any special attention.

Then as the months went by, by sheer effrontery Cleopatra forced her way into at least one section of Roman society.

The real old-fashioned, upper-crust people of course continued to ignore her. But there were certain "new men", jumped-up from the business classes or from the Latin countryside, who were not quite so difficult to lure into the society of an outsider like herself. Men like a certain Marcus Tullius Cicero, for instance, a literary man and one of the greatest Roman lawyers of the day, yet apparently looked-down on by all the best people in Rome.

There were women too, gifted, well educated, intelligent women, but barred from the best society because they were actresses or divorcees, or something or other not acceptable to the old-style Roman matron.

It was not apparently to be expected of a woman that she should possess culture, brains *and* a good character. There was a good deal of head-shaking at the Roman dinner tables just then over the bold and loose behaviour of such modern women; over the shocking amount of adultery and divorce; and over the decline of religion and of public morality.

Like her Roman female guests, Cleopatra could talk freely and well on these and most other topics. But she listened much more than she talked, mindful of the Stoic saying, often quoted by Cicero, though seldom acted upon, "We have two ears but only one mouth; we are therefore meant to listen more than to speak."

Piecing together her dinner-party gleanings, the reports of her paid spies, and the results of her own personal espionage, by the end of that winter Cleopatra had come to a pretty clear understanding of the present political situation in Rome, and some of the personalities involved.

She learned something very alarming: the position of Rome's apparently supreme Dictator was precarious.

Caesar returned from Spain the following September. His campaign had once again been successful, and at first there seemed not a cloud in his sky. Honours were heaped upon him. Another grand triumph was arranged. In the games that followed, a statue of him was carried alongside the statue of Victory. Several other statues were set up in temples about the city. The month Quinctilis was re-named Julius. And now he was proclaimed Perpetual Dictator, not just for a period as before.

"YOU'LL be a king before you're much older," Cleopatra used to say to tease him. And there were many others who either feared or hoped the same thing. Caesar usually became angry at such talk, strongly denying all desire to assume such a title. "My name is Caesar, not Rex!" he would declare.

In February there was a very disturbing incident. It happened at the festival of Lupercalia, a public holiday the Romans held each year in honour of the legendary wolf who suckled Romulus and Remus. Amongst the traditional amusements was a sort of fertility rite, in which the young men of noble birth would run, naked and armed with whips, striking playfully at anybody who got in the way. Women who wished for a child would actually place themselves in the way, for the whips were supposed to be some sort of magic which would help in conception. It was one of Caesar's many official duties to preside over this rite, seated on his golden chair, clad in his purple robes, on the Speakers' platform in the Forum.

To him on this occasion came Mark Antony, his fellow-Consul, who was one of the runners. Pushing through the crowds he offered Caesar a crown wreathed with laurel. At this there was a certain amount of cheering. But there were far louder cheers when Caesar rejected the crown and told Mark Antony to take it to be consecrated at the Capitol.

"I thought Mark Antony was your friend?" said Cleopatra when she heard this. "If so, it was a stupid thing to do, playing into the hands of your enemies! Don't you know that Rome is swarming with your enemies?"

Caesar only smiled.

"A politician can hardly reach my time of life without making a few of those," he declared, so complacently that she completely lost patience.

"Caesar!" she cried. "For Heaven's sake get it into your head that this is serious! There's a whole gang of enemies, vicious enemies, seriously plotting against your life. I could give you the certain names of at least twenty of them, and there are more than that. Men in the highest rank. Why don't you quietly get rid of them, before they can act?"

Noting his look of disdain, she changed her tack.

"Or let me arrange it for you?"

His expression deepened to one of downright disgust.

"No, no, no, Cleopatra. None of your Egyptian stranglings here, please!"

"I don't understand this horror of yours!" declared Cleopatra, knowing well what he was alluding to. "After all, you think nothing of slaying thousands of men in your wars, many of them your own countrymen, your friends even! I've heard you call your legionaries that! 30,000 in Spain, 50,000 in Africa. The gods alone know how many in Gaul and in Asia. All of them 'friends', or at least men who have done you no harm. Then why balk at a dozen or so real enemies, to save your life? You weren't so fastidious when you were young!

What about those pirates you once crucified in revenge for capturing you and demanding ransom?"

"They were crucified not in revenge, but because they were pirates, a menace to Rome on the high seas."

"But such a cruel death! I've seen men dying like that, hundreds of them, all along the Appian Way. Our 'Egyptian strangling' as you call it, is almost kind, compared to that."

"Kind or cruel, Cleopatra, I'll have no man put to death to save *my* life," he declared, very firm and cold. It was clear that this subject was closed.

Cleopatra was silent for a while, then began again from a different angle.

"Caesar," she said, "when I go back to Alexandria, why not come with me? We were so happy together in Egypt, now weren't we?"

"My dear child, I haven't the time for another holiday just now. Rome needs me, desperately."

"I wasn't suggesting a holiday. You could serve Rome just as well from Alexandria. Better in fact. You yourself said it's by far the finer city."

That was a mistake: it pricked his Roman vanity and he smiled quite insultingly.

"My dear Serpent of the Nile," he pointed out. "Alexandria, in fact Egypt itself, wouldn't last long without the Roman legions."

"Then bring your legions with you!" she flashed back.

He laughed aloud at that so that she coloured faintly.

"No, I'm serious, Caesar!" she insisted. "Don't you see it's the perfect combination? In Egypt I am a god, or almost so. My divinity plus your legions: the two together would be irresistible. We could rule the whole world!"

"Thanks, but I shall manage very well without the additional office of Prince Consort of Egypt."

"King of Egypt," she corrected, with all her dignity. "And you admit that you dare not be king, here—and the gods, if you

66

stay and get killed, what will become of me, and our little son?"
she ended, her great eyes suddenly brimming over.

He pulled her on to his knees and kissed her.

"Silly little girl," he told her fondly. "What is there to cry
about? I'm not dead yet. And when I am, you'll get along very
well without your old Caesar."

"But you said yourself that Egypt couldn't last a minute
without the Roman legions," she wept.

"Well, yes. But I shall not be the last of the Romans to be
charmed into being your watch dog!" laughed Caesar, playfully
nibbling her ear-lobe.

Cleopatra's mind seldom lost its edge. Even as her body
responded to his amorousness, she had begun a mental review
of possible future candidates for the office of watch dog, as he
called it.

For it was clear that she had reached the limits of her power
over this man, even supposing he were to escape with his life,
which seemed very unlikely. When he first came back from
Spain he had brought home a personal bodyguard of Spanish
horsemen. But now this was dismissed.

"It's better to die than to go constantly in terror of death," he
declared, and he would insist upon walking unarmed about the
streets of Rome, even at night, as if he were an ordinary citizen.
That was madness, especially as his old weakness, the falling
sickness, had begun to gain upon him recently. How on earth he
had survived through all those wars to the age of fifty-six, Cleopatra could never understand, though it seemed that only once
had he been taken ill in the middle of a battle.

It was clear that her mission had failed. He would never
publicly acknowledge his son Caesarion.

HE HAD made up his mind that the good of Rome would not be
best served by the public acknowledgement of this bastard, as
Caesarion would be in the eyes of all Romans.

Bitter as it was, Cleopatra could see that there was nothing for it but to swallow this knowledge and make her plans to depart as soon as the weather was fit for the long sea journey, perhaps in April?

In any case, Caesar himself would shortly be leaving Rome again. The Parthians were once more giving trouble on the edges of the Roman domains in Asia. Another spell in Rome, without his company, would be quite unbearable as well as unfruitful.

Caesar was not destined to fight the Parthians. The fates had something very different in store for him.

It came about in March, on the day the Romans called the Ides, that is the day of full moon, which fell this month on the fifteenth day.

The morning was very cold. Cleopatra, crouched close to her brazier, was giving Caesarion his daily lesson in the Egyptian tongue, when Charmion came running to them, her eyes big with horror.

"Oh, my lady! Demades—you remember, Caesar's barber— has just come with the most terrible news!"

Cleopatra sprang to her feet, spilling Caesarion from her lap in her instinctive fear.

"They've attacked him?"

Charmion nodded, speechless.

"Is he . . . is he badly wounded?"

"He's dead!"

Silence.

"But, Charmion—only yesterday—last night—" Cleopatra stopped, aware of the little boy's face turned up to her like a small moon, his eyes filling, his lower lip beginning to bulge and quiver.

"Take him to the women and comfort him, and send Demades to me," she said.

Never had Cleopatra seen a man so broken as the little barber. He could hardly see out of his eyes, they were so swollen with weeping. His face was all puckered and crumpled, like a

withered leaf. He was utterly incoherent. She made him sit close
to the brazier, and ordered some warmed sweet wine, mixed
with honey in the Egyptian way.

"Drink this. It will calm you," she commanded.

He obeyed, looking over the rim of the cup in speechless
gratitude as he painfully gulped the liquid.

"Take your time," she said encouragingly, seeing that the
drink was beginning to work. At which he burst out afresh,
sobbing wildly and trying to mop away his tears with the palms
of his hands, like a little boy.

He grew calm at last. The outburst had completed the effect
of the wine, and he began to tell his story, confusedly enough at
first.

"If only he'd listened to his wife! If only he'd listened to
Calpurnia!" he kept saying. "She'd dreamed you see that she
was holding his murdered body in her arms. She woke up crying, and begged him not to go to the Senate today. And you
know Calpurnia was never a superstitious woman. It frightened
him. But that only made him the more bent on going. You
know what he is . . . *was*!"

Cleopatra nodded. "And so he was murdered in the Senate
house?"

"Oh, if only he'd listened! Twenty-three stabs, they say! Oh,
if only he'd—"

"Who did this, Demades?" interrupted Cleopatra, and he
steadied again at her sharpness.

"That fellow Cassius, he was the ringleader they say. And
there was Casca, and Brutus and, oh, a score of others! What
chance had he? Twenty-three of them! Though he put up a
fight. With only his pen for a weapon, he struggled, till he saw
Brutus, the one man he never thought to suspect, though I
could have told him things, if he'd ever listened to me!"

"I too, Demades!"

"But when he saw Brutus, he gave up. Drew his toga over his
face and fell across the foot of that very statue of Pompey he'd
had put up in the Senate House himself. Generous, he was, my

69

master, even to his enemies! And there they finished him off. Twenty-three of them! Oh, my lady, think of it! Twenty-three wounds! One for each . . ."

"Don't! Don't go on so, Demades!" begged Cleopatra, beginning to feel ill as the scene grew in her brain under this torrent of words.

But Demades couldn't seem to stop now.

"I wasn't there," he gabbled on. "I didn't see him die. I only saw that statue afterwards. I ran straight there when they came to the house with the news. I ran with the slaves, old as I am. I saw that statue, all red with his blood, my lady! I walked beside the stretcher and talked to him all the way home—silly old man that I am! No use talking. It was all over by then. The Senate house was empty. They'd all run away, those brave patricians! Stood by—not one hand lifted to help, till it was all over, then bolted to their holes like a pack of frightened rabbits. Not a man amongst 'em!"

"Of course there isn't! How could there be? They've killed the only man in Rome! Their best friend, if they'd had the wit to see it, and my only friend in this terrible place!"

Cleopatra too burst into a passion of weeping, as the full meaning of this dreadful truth reached her heart at last.

That set the barber off again.

"He was all I had in the world!" he wept. "What is there for me in Rome now, my lady, now he's gone? Take me into your service! Take me back with you to Egypt! Away from this slaughter house!"

Cleopatra's emotions were strong, but her will power was stronger still. Quickly recovering, she considered this idea.

What would happen now in Rome? Civil war again, perhaps? Riots, and more bloodshed, almost certainly. It would be very unwise for her to venture into the city just now. But this little old man would be in a splendid position, as a humble member of Caesar's household, to see what was going on. He might be extremely useful to her in keeping her informed.

The poor old creature's gratitude at being made use of in this way was quite pathetic. A born slave, who had resisted several attempts by Caesar to set him free, he was evidently the sort of man who can barely support life without someone to devote himself to. He certainly came in useful to Cleopatra during the period of confusion that followed the murder of Caesar.

The violence she had foreseen did not break out immediately. The common people had revered their Dictator almost as a god. But Brutus was a respected citizen too, whatever the rest of the assassins might be. Ordinary people simply didn't know what to think, or who was in the right. When Brutus spoke in the Forum, vindicating the murder as the just assassination of a dangerous tyrant, the speech was received in silence.

In the Senate, matters were taken in hand by Mark Antony and a man called Lepidus, who had been Caesar's master of horse and governor of parts of Gaul and Spain. With the support of the lawyer Cicero, these two persuaded the Senate to pardon the murderers, but at the same time to decree that Caesar's laws as the late Dictator were to be respected, and his body given a decent burial. For a while it seemed that order would be maintained.

But then Caesar's will was publicly read aloud. It was learned that he had left 300 sesterces to every Roman citizen, and his villa and gardens on the Janiculum for the use of the people. And when the people had seen his mangled corpse in its blood-stained toga being carried through the Forum to be cremated, and had listened to the inflammatory funeral oration of Mark Antony, their feelings broke out into violence.

They stopped the procession (Demades told Cleopatra, who had not dared to be present), smashed up benches and doors from nearby houses, heaped them up in the Forum and burned the corpse there and then.

They then snatched out pieces of blazing wood from the improvised pyre, and ran to set fire to the houses of the assassins, and tear the murderers to pieces. But the murderers were already in hiding in the houses of friends. Brutus and Cassius were soon heard to have fled from Rome, leaving the power in the hands of Mark Antony and Lepidus.

But though the tide seemed to be swinging in favour of Caesar's friends, this did not include Cleopatra. The people, she heard, had thrown down the statue which he had erected in her honour in the temple of Venus. And there were some disturbing rumours as to their intentions concerning Caesar's gardens.

Caesar himself had completely let her down. In his will there had been no mention at all of his son Caesarion. He had named as his chief heir a boy of eighteen, son of his niece Atia, called Octavian.

It was plain to Cleopatra that not only had her mission in Rome completely failed: it had never had a chance of success. For when that will was made, Caesar could not have foreseen the time of his death, could not have foreseen that when it happened Caesarion would still be a mere baby of two and a half. He must never have had the slightest intention of recognising his son as his legal heir.

It was neither safe nor profitable for her to linger on in Rome.

8 Mark Antony

IT was good to be back home, in the land where her own brown people went barefoot and bare-breasted, singing and busy in the fields and on the reedy waters, in the land of colour and song and contentment, where the sun shone all day long and nearly every day, and where pleasant speech rippled like water on the side of a reed-bundle ferry boat.

Not that all was as well as it should have been.

It was Epeiph, the last month of the harvest, when Cleopatra reached Alexandria. But the harvest had not been good, owing to a poor flood last year, attributed, said Intef, to the Queen's absence. Dealers had hoarded so much of the corn that prices rose out of reach of many of the people. Starvation was feared in Alexandria, and in many of the larger cities.

"Yes! I can see it was high time I came home!" thought Cleopatra. And she set to work at once to do what she could to put things right.

Selling many of her personal jewels and treasures, she bought up great quantities of corn and had it distributed cheaply, or even free, to the poorer citizens in Alexandria and Memphis and other centres. She also asked for a survey of the state of the canals. A big programme of new cuttings and embankments, as well as repairs of the old ones, was planned and begun. The management of the tax collectors and of the temple estates, badly run-down and corrupt lately, was tightened and cleaned up to some extent.

The following Inundation Season was a good one. Whether

this was due to all or some of these efforts, or to her mere presence in Egypt, or simply to chance, Cleopatra got the credit for it. Her name was celebrated that year in a thousand temples throughout the kingdom. Much encouraged, she had several representations made of herself and her son, to put into the temple of Dendyra, the crocodile-hating city, and ordered the digging of a new "sacred-lake" for it, fed by the Nile and known as Cleopatra's Pool.

She was beginning to think that she might yet be granted the power and the time to fulfil that vow she had secretly made at her coronation, seven years ago: to be a good mother-goddess to the people of Egypt, to go down in hieroglyphics on the walls of her tomb as one of the great Pharaohs.

At any rate, there was now no rival claim to the throne. Her younger brother had died of some undiagnosed illness, shortly before her return. If only the Romans held off, if only she could hold on until her son came of age!

Perhaps, while those jackals in Rome were snapping and snarling over the carcase of Julius Caesar's kingdom-without-a-king, the kingdom would fall to bits, so that Egypt, in the general chaos, might be able to get along unnoticed with its own business?

Cleopatra kept her eye on events in Rome. She still had a skeleton spy-system there. Other news filtered through via the Jewish community in Alexandria, which had close trade connections with the Roman world.

Rome, she learned, instead of one dictator, now had three: Mark Antony, Octavian (Caesar's great-nephew and heir), and Lepidus, at one time Caesar's Master of Horse. Of course they didn't call themselves dictators. Carefully avoiding this now dirty word, they had taken instead the collective title of "Triumviri", that is, "the rule of three men".

The three between them could command some forty-five legions. But in order to pay all these men, they had begun their reign by ruthlessly hunting down all men known to have shown sympathies to the Republicans, as the murderers of Caesar

called themselves. Three hundred were said to have been executed, and their estates confiscated. Among them was Cicero,
who had rashly spoken out against Antony, in favour of the
old-fashioned Roman Republic. It was said that Antony had
had Cicero's head and hands hung up in the Forum, in revenge
for this opposition: a revenge which seemed to Cleopatra both
barbarous and unnecessary.

Meanwhile Caesar's two chief murderers had fled to Macedonia and Asia Minor, where they were enlisting powerful
armies. Sooner or later they would clash with the "Triumviri"
and so begin one more chapter in this endless civil war, which
with any luck might yet bring Rome to final ruin.

As the Republicans had been responsible for the death of her
only Roman friend, one-time lover, and father of her son, Cleopatra, as a woman, was by nature inclined against them. As a
politician she knew she could not afford such feelings. The
welfare of Egypt, her own security, and that of her son, must
come first. At present the two parties seemed too evenly
matched for it to be prudent to throw in her lot with either.
Remembering her unfortunate misjudgment between Pompey
and Caesar, she would prefer to keep out of it altogether.

Morally there was nothing to choose between them. They
were barbarians and brutes, the whole lot of them. Not one
was fit to wash the feet of Julius Caesar. Ruthless Caesar may
have been, splendidly ruthless, when necessary. But merciful too,
whenever it was possible. Not one of these men knew the meaning of mercy. They were not big enough. Well, let them murder each other to their hearts' content. The longer they kept at
it, the better for Egypt.

But this state of affairs did not last as long as she would have
liked. When the second Inundation after her return (another
good one, fortunately) had come and gone, and the land was
busy under the plough and the sowers, there came news of a
decisive battle near Philippi in Macedonia.

"Isn't it strange?" remarked Cleopatra to Intef, "how often

75

these Romans manage to fight out their quarrels over other people's lands?"

The victory, it seemed, had gone to Octavian and Mark Antony, and Cassius and Brutus had committed suicide.

It was Mark Antony, in fact, who had been chiefly responsible for the victory. Octavian had been vanquished by Brutus at first, and later, taken very ill, had left the battle in Antony's hands and been carried back to Rome, not expected to live very long. And now Antony was marching southwards into Greece, and reputed to be living it up at a very high rate, with harpers and pipers, dancers and buffoons, spending money as fast as he could rake it in from the submissive Greek citizens. To be sure, not all was spent on his own extravagant self. A good deal of it was for his men. Every common soldier in his legions was said to have been promised 5,000 drachmas for a victorious campaign.

Despite these extortions he seemed to be welcomed everywhere, especially in Athens, where he flattered the citizens by hearing their learned philosophers dispute, watching athletic contests, and undergoing civic initiation.

It was the same when he crossed over into Asia. On his entry into Ephesus, for instance, he was met by a wild procession of women dressed like bachantes, and men and boys like satyrs, dancing to the music of harps and flutes, and addressing him in song as Bacchus, god of wine and "bringer of joy".

The last detail amused Cleopatra greatly. When she was in Rome Mark Antony had been notorious for his eager appreciation of the pleasures of Bacchus, and indeed all other fleshly joys.

"Though I never heard, Charmion," she remarked with a laugh, "that he laid claim to *this* particular divinity. I understood he was descended from Hercules!"

"Joking apart, I think the present situation is better, from Egypt's point of view," was her final judgment.

She would of course have preferred a stalemate for years to come. But still, with one of the contestants so sick that he might oblige everyone by dying, and others safely dead, there was really only Mark Antony left to reckon with.

Besides, he was said to be preparing for a terrible campaign again the Parthians. That would keep him out of mischief for some time to come. Even the Romans had never yet been able to master those Parthians!

THE FOLLOWING SPRING Cleopatra was brought several letters from Mark Antony, commanding her in very peremptory terms to come to him in Tarsus and account for the help she had given to Cassius in the recent civil war. That was nonsense, of course. She had deliberately kept clear of all that, and Antony well knew it.

Then what did he want? Was he trying to pick a quarrel to have the excuse of invading Egypt?

One of Antony's envoys, a man called Dellius, assured her very earnestly that she had nothing to fear. No treachery whatever was in his master's mind. He advised her to go. The general was by nature as easy as anyone could be with a woman.

Dellius seemed to her honest enough, the blunt, crop-haired kind of veteran soldier she had learned to know and respect in Rome. Besides, there was certainly something in what he said.

"They say Mark Antony's wife, Fulvia, can run rings round him. And she's a proper old frump. We saw her in Rome, do you remember? So surely I can manage him?" she said to Charmion.

Finally Cleopatra made up her mind to go to Tarsus, but in her own good time, after a dignified time-lag, and as if at her own pleasure.

About a month later, the citizens of Tarsus were amazed to see a gorgeous and exotic vessel rowed up their river, a vessel with a stern elaborately carved and gilded, a prow shaped and painted to look like a large but graceful lotus blossom, a purple sail, and oars of silver, moving to weird music played on flutes and harps. Except for the oarsmen, it seemed to be "manned" by women, or rather, to judge from their scanty gauzy green garments, by sea-nymphs.

Amidships, under a fringed canopy of gold and purple, lay the most beautiful creature ever seen, her body in the flimsiest of gold-gauze draperies, her huge black eyes slanting like a cat's, her hair dressed in a thousand tiny ringlets, each ending in a jewel, and her head bearing a strange ornament, rather like a horned moon with a full moon between.

"It is a goddess!" the people of Tarsus cried, and more and more of them crowded to the river side to see this amazing sight.

The river Cydnus ran right through the middle of the city, and was both narrow and swift. There was hardly a breath of air, and the purple sail was of little use, which was perhaps as well, as the sea-nymph-crew seemed none too seamanlike. The oarsmen, toiling hard in perfect time to the harps, made slow progress against the current. There was ample time for the news to spread. Long before the vessel had reached the city wharves, nearly all the people of Tarsus had gathered along the river banks, pushing and struggling to get a good view, and shouting "Aphrodite! It's Aphrodite! Aphrodite's come to Tarsus!"

Cleopatra smiled as she heard that. She had not actually meant to represent herself as the Greek goddess of love and beauty. Her galley was simply the usual ceremonial vessel of a Pharaoh. Her costume was her own modified version of the costume of Isis, the Egyptian Mother of the Gods. But these people of course knew nothing of the gods of Egypt. And "Aphrodite" would do very well for her purpose!

"This will teach him to send for me as if I were a prisoner at the bar," she told herself.

At the time of her arrival, of which she had sent no word to Antony, he happened to be presiding over a court of justice in the Forum of the town. By the time Cleopatra's vessel was moored the market place was virtually empty.

"What in the name of Hercules is going on?" he asked at

last, turning to the native interpreter who had been explaining the cases to him.

The man returned after a lengthy interval, for it had been difficult to find any citizen to question, nearer than the docks.

"The Queen of Egypt has arrived, and the people believe it is Aphrodite, come to feast with the god Bacchus," he reported.

Antony burst out laughing.

"And so she shall, by Bacchus, so she shall!" he cried.

Sending the man right back to the wharf with a cordial invitation to Cleopatra to join him at supper that very night, he hurried away to his quarters to make ready.

Halfway through his preparations came the reply. The Queen of Egypt thanked him for his kindness, but begged to be excused. She was tired after the long voyage and would prefer that they meet aboard her own vessel for a quiet informal meal, which in fact was already in preparation when *his* invitation arrived. She hoped this would be no inconvenience.

Again Antony burst into laughter, not quite so hearty as before, but good-natured enough.

"Ah well, must humour the ladies, eh, Dellius?" was all he said to his aide-de-camp, as with a shrug of his broad shoulders he countermanded all his recent orders.

"A quiet informal meal", Cleopatra had called it. What then would she have laid on for a real state banquet? Mark Antony was used to some luxury, if not downright extravagance, in his style of living, but he had never met anything like the entertainment provided on the Egyptian galley.

It was no vulgar ostentation either. Everything was elegant, from food to slaves, and the food was fit for the gods he and she were popularly supposed to be!

He had always heard that the Egyptians were good at bread-making. But he had never seen such a variety of fancy breads and cakes, all equally tasty, with ginger and all sorts of unknown eastern spices. The meat dishes were even better, especially a roast duck (the Egyptians were famous for their water birds) with a sauce which got caught in his beard, but was well worth that inconvenience.

And she had had the good sense, he was thankful to find, to bring not those terrible Egyptian wines, but the best Greek ones.

He helped himself freely, though not to more than he could carry. It took a good deal to get Antony really drunk.

His hostess drank sparingly but with an air of freedom which delighted him. Roman women were brought up to believe that drinking was unfeminine, and when they did take to it could neither do it gracefully nor hold their liquor.

On close inspection he decided the Queen of Egypt was by no means an Aphrodite. The citizens of Tarsus must have been dazzled by the golden trappings. But she was a fine figure of a woman, with a marvellous pair of eyes and a voice like a hive of humming bees. Damned good company too.

"Why in Hades did you have to waste yourself on Julius Caesar?" he demanded at one point, "Couldn't you wait for me?"

"Ah! If I'd only known, Mark Antony!" she responded, with a mocking, provocative smile.

The sun went down and the stars came out. Presently Cleopatra's people lowered from the galley-rigging, on cleverly improvised candelabras, the prettiest set of lights he had ever seen, all arranged in circles and triangles like a Euclid in lamplight. Under this arbour they ate and drank far into the night. And not a word all this time of Cassius.

Next day came Antony's turn to entertain.

"But don't expect anything like this!" he warned her as he took his leave, sometime in the small hours. "I can't hope to equal your hospitality. But I will do my poor best as a rough soldier on campaign!"

Poor Antony! Almost everything went wrong. The meats were tough. The broth was cold. The desert was stringy. The bread might have been made for the Jewish feast of the Passover. The slaves were awkward, even insolent at times. He was too familiar with them, and they took advantage of it, as slaves will.

But he laughed it all off as a huge joke, without a trace of embarrassment, enjoying himself as before. By the time the evening was done, he was half drunk, not with wine, but with love, or at any rate with desire. His eyes openly declared the fact.

She for her part found him not unattractive. She was used to clean-shaven men, of course, but she was quite taken by his short brown bushy beard, proclaiming his supposed descent from Hercules. His nose was too prominent, and his whole face too long between eyes and mouth. His body, though inclined to portliness, was still very fine. But there was something else beyond mere looks, a warmth and spontaneity of the spirit, which was really very likeable.

However, if they were to be lovers, it would be for her chiefly a business transaction. What, she wondered, as she laughed, and talked, and met his interested eyes boldly, look for look, what was there in it for her and for Egypt?

Mark Antony was no Caesar. But neither was he a fool. He might even yet end up as the ruler, if not of the whole Roman world, at least of the eastern half of it. Wasn't it the obvious thing to do to gain his goodwill, to manoeuvre him into the part of Egypt's ally, while his own final destiny was still unproven, rather than just sit waiting until he was lord of all the rest of the world and could swallow Egypt like a sweetmeat?

This man, brilliant in war no doubt, was as wax in the hands of a clever woman. It should not be difficult to make him her tool, and Egypt's. Perhaps, she dreamed, it might even end in Rome itself becoming the vassal of the Queen of Egypt?

But that was looking too far ahead! For the present her task was so to bewitch this general that he would come to think of Egypt and herself as one, and of Egypt as his ally, not his victim.

She felt her success sure if she chose to do this. Antony was easy game compared to Caesar, upon whom she had worked by sheer instinct, and to whom her very girlishness had been a great part of the charm. Now she was seven years older, working from experience upon a man still in his prime.

Long before her galley slid down the Cydnus again, Mark Antony was completely infatuated, and had given his solemn promise to visit her in Egypt as soon as he had finished in Asia Minor.

Incidentally she had used him to do a useful piece of tidying up. Without even deigning to refer to the accusation which had brought her to Tarsus, she one day mentioned, casually, that her sister Arsinoe, now in sanctuary in some temple in Rome, had had dealings with Cassius.

"I imagine she must be on your list of traitors," she remarked.

He realised her meaning at once.

"We must have overlooked her. But I can soon put that right," he said coolly. She knew he would keep his word, and that would be the end of Arsinoe. Not that the Crocodile was likely to have made any more trouble. But you never knew. Just as well to get her out of the way while there was a chance.

9 *Fig Leaves and Oranges*

WHEN Julius Caesar had set foot in Alexandria, seven years before, he had all the insignia of authority as a Roman Consul, the lictors carrying before him the double-headed axe and faggots, symbol of the Roman state. When Mark Antony arrived, he came simply as a man and as Cleopatra's private guest. It was a measure of the difference in the two men, and of the increased stability of Cleopatra's position.

He soon made himself thoroughly at home in Alexandria. In fact, before many weeks had passed his behaviour had become notorious throughout Egypt. Amongst the pleasure-loving élite of the city he set up a sort of club, which he called "The Inimitable Livers", whose members competed with each other in their extravagant entertainment. Taking it in turns to be host, these people would go out in small boats along the canal to Canopus, the suburb of Alexandria where religious festivals took place. It was a well-known haunt of dancing girls and acrobats, singers and musicians and actors, not to mention criminals and prostitutes. Hardly a day passed in Canopus without some sort of religious, or pseudo-religious, revelry. The air was filled with flutes and harps and the drunken shouts and screams of the revellers.

Not only here, but in all parts of the city, the queen and her guest were frequently to be seen: at the theatre, hippodrome, or athletic displays. Chariot races bored Cleopatra, and athletics were by no means her favourite entertainment. Like most of her people, the one form of manly exercise which she understood well enough to enjoy was wrestling. But Antony delighted in all such things, and even took part in athletics himself. To please him she cultivated a certain enthusiasm. He had, after all, a very fine body, and even in competition with much younger men his performance was by no means disgraceful.

He was fond of fishing and hunting too. She had to spend many a day with her guest, duck-hunting among the reed beds of the Delta or on Lake Mareotis, just south of the city, where he insisted upon trying his hand with that ancient Egyptian fowling weapon, the boomerang. It was an impossible weapon for those not born and bred to it. Antony's performance was quite farcical.

There was, indeed, something of the born clown in him, and there were times when Cleopatra sighed for the seriousness of his predecessor, for the stimulating contact of that active and curious mind. But Antony was such good company, so much more fun as a lover. With a wider experience of women, warmer by temperament, more frank and more generous, he knew so much better how to please in love. And he never cared what he did or said, or where, or what sort of a figure he cut.

Somewhat to Cleopatra's surprise therefore, what had begun simply as a business proposition, or to put it crudely, an act of State-prostitution, soon became a pleasure for its own sake. She did not exactly love Antony, at any rate at first. But to have him as her lover was by no means disagreeable.

By the middle of the winter the relationship had gone much further than this. There was of course no mention of marriage. After her experience with Caesar she took care to make no such mistake with this second Roman. But there was a familiarity, an ease, a sort of habitual fondness in Antony's attitude that seemed to her to belong to the married man, rather than to the passing lover. And in Egyptian eyes this *was* a marriage, just as the association with Caesar had been a marriage.

Unlike Caesar, Antony's love showed no sign of cooling when she became pregnant. A certain vein of prudery, or perhaps merely of fastidiousness, which had appeared in Caesar at this stage, seemed lacking in Antony's nature.

Once at a public banquet after a long religious ceremony, during which her legs had become painfully swollen because of her condition, he massaged them in front of all the court, to the general scandal, but to her complete delight. Momentarily at least, she genuinely loved him; she loved him for his magnificent disregard of public opinion.

Often, as her body grew heavier, he would lift her up, and stagger clownishly about the room with her in his arms, and pretend to drop her.

"Why, there must be a whole legion of little Antonys in there!" he would exclaim, as he set her down and patted her stomach with a droll look. (She was considerably bigger than when carrying Caesar's child and sometimes wondered if she were carrying twins.)

Far from betraying any embarrassment on account of his responsibility for her pregnancy, he bragged freely and loudly of this and other exploits, several times comparing himself to Caesar, to the latter's disadvantage.

"Three wives—four, counting you!" he would say, "and he only sired this one little Egyptian lad from the lot! He had to leave his fortune to a great-nephew! It's pathetic, isn't it? Now me, I could breed them by the dozen! Just wait till I start in earnest!"

Yes, it was pleasant enough to have Mark Antony around as unofficial husband, and she was by no means sorry to be with child again. One child was after all a frail sort of insurance against the future. But where was all this leading?

She had intended Mark Antony for her tool. He was to have been working for her and for Egypt out in the Roman world, not playing the clown, however agreeably, in the suburbs of Alexandria. She began to wonder if, after all, she was backing the wrong chariot. She had calculated that this man would be wax in her hands. Was he after all more unmanageable than she had thought? Or was he perhaps all *too* wax-like, with no will or ambition of his own?

One day when they were out fishing she tried to drop a hint on this matter.

Restless and impatient by nature, Antony, though he loved the sport, was no great fisherman. He had done badly the day before, and on this occasion, to make a better show, had bribed some Egyptian boys to dive in and fix fish to his hooks. Cleopatra quickly spotted the trick, and to tease him got one of the boys to fix on a piece of salted fish. There were roars of laughter when Antony drew this up, but as usual he took it in very good part.

"Why do you waste yourself on fishing? Leave that to the poor Queen of Egypt. Your game is with cities and provinces and kingdoms!" Cleopatra told him archly. He took that well, too: too well, perhaps. If he had taken offence it might have been a better omen, she felt.

However, in the spring when the seas once more opened to shipping and news could travel, despatches came which stirred Antony at last out of this marital indolence.

He had left Syria and Asia Minor last autumn, as he thought, in a state of reasonable calm and order, with reliable puppet-kings installed in various small kingdoms, and two legions policing Syria. But now it seemed that an ex-officer of the dead Cassius, Quintus Labienus, had gone to the court of the King of the Parthians and persuaded the King's son, Pacorus, to make war with him on Antony's troops. The two legions had deserted to Labienus, who was marching across Asia Minor; while Pacorus had taken all Syria except for the city of Tyre, which was built on an island. It was plain that Antony was urgently needed. And as soon as his ship could be manned and equipped, he left.

Cleopatra was half glad and half uneasy. It was a relief that he could be in action again. But once out of her sight, would his actions necessarily work for the benefit of Egypt? She felt far from certain of that.

After all the time she had spent in his company, she still had very little clue as to what was in his mind. Was it even certain that Mark Antony *had* a mind? Or was he just a splendid warm-blooded animal?

THERE was a smell of sun-warmed fig leaves and ripe oranges. Between the water lilies a few fish were beginning to nose out their evening rings. On the far side of the pool Caesarion was throwing corn to his pet pigeons. He called them all by name, and they came flocking about his bare feet, jerking their necks and cooing excitedly. Lying on their backs in the shade of the persimmon tree were the twins, jerking their arms and legs, doubling their fat chins, and making noises remarkably like those of the pigeons.

It was an idyllic scene, Cleopatra supposed. But, dare she admit it to herself?—just a little bit of a bore. Was it a symbol of her life in general?

Her kingdom was prosperous enough, contented enough, like the fluttering pigeons. There was no doubt about that. Money talks, and the recent estimates of the taxes which the country could afford to pay next year were proof enough in themselves. There had been an exceptionally good inundation, and there would probably be an equally rich harvest. In fact, never since her return from Rome had the inundation fallen below the "cubits of death", as they called the lowest height necessary to feed the population.

To the common people, that was all her doing. She was their mother-goddess, the incarnation of Isis, or of the even older cow-goddess, Hathor. Their faith in this had deepened since the birth of the twins and since her frequent public appearances with one or other, or both, in her arms.

But the focus of a nation's religious emotions means more for the worshippers than for the worshipped. This she had long ago discovered, in the performance, day after day, year after year, of the ancient rituals which were to ensure the continued life and prosperity of these worshipping millions.

Even worse was the crushing burden of administration, that treadmill of paper, which she always felt would turn as well without her, yet which just *didn't*.

And she was still only twenty-nine! There would be years and years of it yet, before any of the children were old enough to begin to take some of the burden off her back.

And what of all those wild dreams of hers—of further glory and conquest for the land of Egypt, as in the times of the great Thothmes? For these she needed a man, a fighter, a great general. Where should she find any such man? Caesar was dead, and Antony a slippery customer, an eel.

What was he up to at this moment? He had left her, he claimed, in order to fight back the Parthians from Asia Minor. He had done nothing of the kind. For the last six months, so far as she had heard, he had been marking time in Greece for some mysterious reason.

Had she backed the wrong man? Intef thought so. Only the other day he had urged that Octavian was the man of the future, not Mark Antony. But what was the good of telling her that? "First catch your duck," is an old, old phrase.

Someday perhaps Caesarion . . . ?

Cleopatra watched her son for a moment or two, jumping up and down, a little wooden puppet amongst the strutting pigeons. Her heart sank.

How fragile he looked, weedy, almost. His brown body, bare except for his loin-cloth, was thin as a weasel's. He was still not quite eight. But even for eight he was certainly under-sized, and very childish mentally. There were times when, to her dismay, he reminded her of her brothers at a similar age.

But not by his nature, though. Just at this moment for instance, hearing one of the babies set up a wail, he abandoned the pigeons and went running to see what was wrong, though the nursemaid was at hand. Squatting in the dappled shade, snapping his fingers and smacking his lips, he had soon turned the wail into a fat chuckle.

The lad seemed to have cast himself in the role of uncle to these new arrivals. Not a trace of jealousy had he shown from the first—which was unbelievable in a son of the Ptolemies!

But where, on the other hand, was the Caesar in him? "Is it conceivable that this affectionate, gentle little creature will ever grow up to be the son of such a father?" she was asking herself, when she saw Intef coming across the garden. A secretary walked behind him, carrying a rolled and sealed letter.

"More state business!" she thought morosely. "Can I never be free, even the last hour before sunset, to sit with my children like any ordinary mother?"

Then she saw that the seal was Antony's. And her heavy mood slipped from her like a cloak.

"Ah, from Athens?" she cried eagerly, almost snatching the roll from the secretary's grasp.

"No, madam. From Brundisium. The ship came in barely an hour ago," Intef corrected her, then stood by politely but inquisitively as she broke the seal and began to read the first lines from Mark Antony since his departure in the spring.

Presently he saw her change colour, suddenly and violently. As she lifted her eyes from the letter, Intef cowered back under her rage.

"He's married, Intef! The rotten stinking hound is married!"

"But we knew that before; we knew all about Fulvia."

"Fulvia my foot! She's dead. He's married again. And of all women, to marry Octavia, Octavian's half sister! Oh the . . . he could not have thought of anything worse!"

"Ah, I begin to see . . ." nodded Intef with an infuriating air of wisdom. Cleopatra cut in furiously:

"That's more than *I* do! Listen! Listen to this!"

She remembered the hovering secretary, waved him angrily out of ear-shot, and in a trembling voice read the letter out aloud to Intef.

" 'Queen of my heart . . .' Pah! Queen of his little toe more like! 'Queen of my heart—I know that you are really a political animal, with the brain of a man. I therefore hope that you will not take my news like a woman. It had to be done, my queen. Political considerations forced me to take Octavia as my wife.

" 'Fulvia, as you will not perhaps have heard, died three months ago in Greece. It was just as well. She was dangerous, and very nearly ruined me: she fancied herself an Amazon and went to war with Octavian, on *my* behalf if you please!

" 'However, Octavian and I have patched things up, and unfortunately one of the patches is Octavia.

" 'Queen of Beauty, there was no other way, I swear to you! I could do nothing in Asia without my troops from Gaul, which Octavian had his claws on. There was trouble in Macedonia too, and there also I had no troops to hand.

" 'Well, we have come to terms again. I am still master of the East, he of the West. My legions, or some of them, are my own again.

" 'The situation is still tricky, too complicated to explain by letter. That must wait until our next meeting.

" 'Cleopatra, my heart's blood, I love you as dearly as ever. I long to see you and hold you in my arms again and will do so as early as fate will allow me. Take care of yourself in the meantime, and of our dear children. I was delighted to hear of *that*. Yes, name them Alexander and Cleopatra, as you wish. Both excellent names! Farewell—and remember, I love you.'

"Love!" cried Cleopatra bitterly, "as if I care for that! He could get himself a heaven full of houris for all I cared! But to marry Octavia! Don't you see, Intef, this means he's abandoned me, and the Eastern Empire we were to share? He's thrown in his lot now with Octavian."

"If he has," said Intef, "I feel it's an error of judgment. They tell me Octavian is one of the wiliest politicians in Rome. And it's politics that count in the long run."

"What's more, Intef, I feel in my bones that Octavian will never rest until there's not three, but one Dictator in Rome—Octavian! It's not a bit of good trying to placate him. Antony will have to fight it out in the end. Well!" she ended grimly, "Just let him come running here for help, when that time comes! He'll find I shall drive a harder bargain next time!"

10 *The Parthians*

IT was three years before Cleopatra met Antony again. This time it was in Antioch. His bushy beard was sprinkled with grey now. But otherwise he was just the same, boisterous and hopeful, careless and good-humoured, swaggering in his short rough cloak showing off his still good figure, imagining himself the reincarnation of Hercules, hob-nobbing with his adoring troops, grabbing and handing out money with equal readiness, and as much in love with her as ever.

His account of his recent marriage seemed plausible enough: a genuine political move, made simply to avoid a head-on clash with Octavian.

It had been touch and go three years ago, he said, whether war was to break out between them. Fulvia, it seemed, had strongly urged him to make an alliance with a rebel and outlaw called Ahenobarbus, one of Caesar's murderers, and with a man called Sextus Pompeius, a son of Pompey's, a sort of pirate king who was interfering with Octavian's corn supplies off the coast of Sicily.

"I half meant to take her advice," Antony said. "I was so mad when I was kept out of Brundisium by Octavian's orders, or so I imagined. But the troops and Octavia patched things up. They were sick to death of civil wars. And so am I for that matter. Where do they get a man, after all? In the name of Hercules! We don't want all the world! If Octavian will leave us in peace, you and I will be well content with half a world, will we not, my queen?"

He gave Cleopatra one of his crushing hugs. She extricated herself with smiling dignity.

"But did the bargain have to include the man's sister?" she said.

For although her personal resentment had quickly evaporated in the warmth of Antony's welcome, she had decided for political reasons to maintain a pretended grievance.

Antony was the easiest man in the world for this sort of game.

"Oh come, I've explained that! Purely a political liaison, I swear it!" he protested.

"And your two daughters, and the child she's carrying now—political progeny?"

"Well, hang it, the mere form of a marriage wouldn't have done, you know. I had to consummate it!"

"Three times over?"

He reddened perceptibly at this.

"Hercules! I may be a political animal, but I'm still a—"

"*Animal?*" she filled in neatly. Antony roared with laughter at that, as usual too good-natured to resent a good joke against himself. "But I can assure you, my love," he resumed after a moment, "there was precious little pleasure in it! Oh, she's very noble and all that. The soul of honour and wifely and sisterly duty. A real old style Roman matron. But oh, so dull. Ha! She thought she had me tamed and caged into a respectable Roman pater! Toga'd up to the chin and a regular attender of philosophical lectures at the Athenian Academy! I swear by the gods, I couldn't have stood it another month. The outcome wasn't what I'd hoped for in any case. I was positively glad of the excuse to pack that prig of a woman back to Rome!"

"So now you've broken with Octavian?" Cleopatra fastened on the one item here which really concerned her.

"Not openly. But it's hopeless to go on trying to pacify such a man. He's snubbed me over and over again. Called me across the sea from Greece with all my ships, to help him against Sextus Pompeius, and then told me to my face he could do

CLEOPATRA

without me. We nearly came to blows over that. Octavia
alone prevented it. She's a born diplomatist. But now he's
cheated again. He's had one hundred and twenty of my ships,
and was to have let me have four extra legions for the Parthian
war. I've never seen one boot of those legions! No! I've done
with Octavian and his ice-maiden. From now on, you and I will
build a great empire in the East. To Hades with the rest! What
do you say, my Queen of Beauty?"

"I'll do what I can to help you," said the Queen of Beauty
guardedly.

"Come off it!" laughed Antony. "Hercules! If I could only
make you see how glad I am to be rid of them all and back in
your arms!"

He pulled her on to his knee and kissed her.

Whatever his value as a political ally, Mark Antony was
irresistible as a man. She did not resist. But as she had vowed to
Intef, she drove a harder bargain this time.

Antony was made to promise that as soon as it was prudent
to defy Octavian ("When I've got the Parthians beaten and rule
in the East") he would divorce Octavia and marry Cleopatra,
Roman-style. In the meantime, he must acknowledge her as his
"Egyptian wife", and the twins as his own lawful progeny and
heirs to his estate. He made a will to that effect, and sent it to
be filed in the archives of the Vestal Virgins in Rome, where
such documents were traditionally kept.

As a wedding present she asked Antony to hand over certain
territories at present in Roman hands, but once part of the
domains of Egypt: Cyprus, Coele-Syria, the coast of Palestine
and part of Cilicia, the valuable forests of the Taurus to provide
timber for ships, always a great problem for Egypt, where trees
were so scarce.

She wanted Judaea too. But Antony had recently placed
King Herod there as a puppet king. As a compromise he
granted her the use of the balsam gardens of Jericho, and of the
bitumen beds east of the Dead Sea.

94

In return, she promised to do all that she could to help to finance the campaign against the Parthians.

She had little sympathy for this enterprise, seeing no benefit for Egypt. But like other Roman generals before him, Antony saw the Parthians both as a menace and as a challenge. Twice in the last two years they had been beaten. But they had never been properly crushed: after each defeat they simply retreated behind the Euphrates to gather strength again.

However, winter was coming. It would be unwise to venture into the wilds of Parthia until the spring. He would spend the winter in Antioch.

This city, at the junction of ancient military and trade routes between Egypt, Asia Minor, and Mesopotamia, was an obvious choice as a campaign base. It was also a very fine city, not as magnificent as Alexandria, but beautifully laid out on a site between the river Orontes and the mountains; a four-hundred-year-old city of many races, living together in harmony, all legally equal, with an elected common council; a city with a very agreeable winter climate, even to one accustomed to the winter sunshine of Alexandria.

Antony had many preparations to make. But as usual he took things easily, and all through that winter he and his reconciled Egyptian wife were to be seen everywhere together in "four-citied Antioch", with their three-year-old twins and Caesarion, whom Antony treated as his own son.

He was fond of most children, and doted on his twins. He was often to be seen in the streets with a child riding on each shoulder, pulling unmercifully at his curls by way of reins. "My sun and my moon" he proudly called them. And in fact they were now known officially as "Alexander Helios" (Sun) and "Cleopatra Selene" (Moon). They were a pretty pair, nearly identical in spite of being boy and girl, plump, full of vitality like both parents, and lamentably spoilt, not only by their father but by the Roman troops.

During that winter Cleopatra came to understand more clearly than ever before just what kind of man she had to deal with: a man to whom pleasure and self-indulgence of every kind, innocent or not so innocent, meant far more than fame: a man in whom ambition erupted only at irregular intervals, like the volcano of Vesuvius.

At the same time, so handsome, so vital, so warm, so generous, and such good fun, he was a man impossible to resist. In the spring, when she and her children returned to Alexandria, she was again pregnant.

They all went with Antony across to the north east of Coele-Syria, now "her'" territory. From here he planned to march through Armenia, whose king was now allied to Rome after a recent defeat by one of Antony's generals. After Armenia, he would make for Phraaspa, the capital of the Medes, and from there push on, perhaps this year, perhaps next, to Ecbatana, the capital of the Parthians.

Cleopatra and her children travelled back by way of Judaea to visit Herod, who had greatly resented her wedding gift of the balsam gardens. Partly by persuasion and partly by veiled bullying (for he knew well that his throne and life depended on Antony's favour and therefore on hers) she got him to lease them back from her for two hundred talents a year.

A similar deal was arranged with Malchus, the previous owner of the bitumen fields near the Dead Sea (valuable to Egypt for many purposes, including the processing of corpses into mummies). Herod moreover, was forced into an agreement to guarantee this second deal, and even collect the two hundred talents for the bitumen beds, and send them on to her.

She reached Alexandria rather pleased with the results of her trip to Antioch.

FOR months there was no news at all from Parthia. News could travel fairly easily to Egypt along the coast from Syria, and even from the sea-towns of Asia Minor. But Antony was away in the interior of Asia, far beyond the Black Sea and the

Euphrates river. It was well-nigh impossible for him to communicate with Cleopatra.

Not until Choiak, the month of the longest nights, did his first despatch reach Egypt.

The campaign was over, a complete failure, almost a catastrophe, he told her. Not for the first time, by their semi-guerrilla tactics, and the wild nature of their land, the Parthians had routed the highly disciplined legions of Rome. Antony had lost nearly half his men. The survivors were in a lamentable condition. Could she come to their rescue with reinforcements, money, food, clothing and equipment? He had brought the remnants to a small place on the coast of Palestine, called the White Village, not daring to make for a large town in case the Parthians had taken the whole of Syria. However, they appeared to have retreated now to their own country. It would be safe enough for her to meet him there.

Cleopatra's heart sank. Was Antony after all to prove an utterly useless tool even at the war-game? Was he even going to be a liability?

But she had pledged herself to support him in return for the wedding settlements. She could not, in decency, fail him altogether at this very first set-back.

Reinforcements, he said. Well no—that was not possible. Egypt had no army to speak of. From time immemorial it had been next to hopeless to make soldiers out of the Egyptian peasants. The Macedonian mercenaries brought in by the Ptolemies were all very well when fresh to the country. But sooner or later they married Egyptian girls and became fainthearted farmers.

Money? Oh no— she could not possibly hand out money from the Egyptian treasury, in unlimited quantities, to make up for losses in a campaign which was of no profit to Egypt, and of which she had never approved. Twenty-eight dinars per soldier she would give, and not a sesterce more.

Food, clothing and equipment she could give in plenty. And she would go with the transport ship herself. She was not at all

97

well, having barely recovered from the birth of her fourth child. And it would be a dangerous voyage, even along the coast, being in mid-winter. But she wanted to hear what had happened from Antony's own lips, and try to weigh up for herself how much was due to misfortune and how much to his own mismanagement.

She found her lover physically much changed, haggard, sunken-eyed, alarmingly thin and markedly greyer, yet by no means abject.

Not that he sought to disguise the extent of his failure, or of his own responsibility for it.

"I made three big mistakes right at the start," he admitted frankly. "First of all, by not waiting in Armenia at the end of the summer. I should have had the foresight to go into winter quarters and carry on again in the spring. I thought I could get it all mopped up by the end of the autumn. But winter comes early in those parts. And ye gods! *What* a winter!

"Mistake number two—leaving my siege equipment in the rear. Three hundred waggon loads of it! Including my best battering ram, eighty feet long. Mind you, my waggon commander is a good chap, and he had a detachment of over 10,000 men. But he wasn't sharp enough for the Parthians. Their king sent a strong body of horse (they're marvellous horsemen) took him by surprise, and cut the detachment to bits. I needed that siege stuff badly before long. I must have been out of my mind to dream of taking the Median capital without it. The trees in those parts are mere sticks. You couldn't make a *toy* ram out of 'em!

"Mistake number three, to put my trust in that damned Artavasdes—king of Armenia, you know. Pah! He wasn't worth the papyrus he signed his name on! As soon as he hears of the waggon fiasco, off he scuttles, like the rat he is! I'm too trusting. I'm a man that keeps his word, and so I always expect the other fellow will keep his. I'm let down time after time. Yes—too trusting, that's my weakness."

And too frank, Cleopatra privately thought.

"It doesn't do," she said to Charmion that night, "for a leader of men to talk about his mistakes so freely to everybody."

But this did not seem to be true, so far as Antony's army was concerned. On the contrary, the men seemed to adore him all the more for his defeat.

Cleopatra talked to many of the survivors herself, and was astonished by the devotion with which they spoke of him, some with tears pouring down their battle-scarred cheeks, as they described his unfailing fortitude all through that terrible retreat over the mountains of Media: how on the night after the worst defeat of all, he had gone selflessly from tent to tent, comforting the wounded and the sick, doing everything he could for their welfare, himself exhausted, often in tears, in his grief for their distress, and his shame for his own responsibility for it.

"He's a man like ourselves, is our general! It's easy to die for a general like our Mark Antony!" they would declare with almost religious fervour.

These men had gone through Hell: twenty-seven days of it, marching by night and day, perpetually harassed at the rear, bewildered, ambushed and starved. At one point they had virtually no provisions left. The baggage horses were either dead, or in use for carrying the sick and wounded. It was a poor country, furnishing little corn. What they did get they had no means of grinding. They had to resort to unfamiliar plants found by the way.

One such plant proved fatal. Those that ate it turned senseless, roaming about and aimlessly moving stones from one place to another. In the end they vomited horribly and died.

At another time some drank from a stream which not only failed to slake their thirst, but gave them agonising pains in the bowels.

Those twenty-seven days were not the end of Hell. When they had at last crossed the river Araxes, out of reach of the Parthians, there was still a weary march through Armenia, in bitter snow storms, in which a further 8,000 men lost their lives.

Altogether about 28,000 infantry and at least 4,000 cavalry

had perished on this luckless adventure. Yet men and officers alike all praised Antony's courage and decision in bringing the rest through the ordeal.

"None of us would be here today if it hadn't been for the general," her old friend Dellius assured her. "I don't believe there's another man who could have got us out alive."

They seemed to forget that they would never have been in Parthia at all if he had not taken them there. Surely, thought Cleopatra, there must be real greatness in a man who could fill his followers with such adoration that they could not see so obvious a fact?

SPRING returned. Lazing on the seashore in the warm sunshine, eating the good food from Egypt, the battered army, its commander, and their Egyptian benefactress, gradually recuperated.

One day a letter arrived for Antony from Rome. He read it rapidly and carelessly, burst out laughing, and tossed it into Cleopatra's lap.

"Epistle from the perfect Roman wife! Read it! Nothing private!" he told her.

It seemed that Octavia was on her way out east, bringing, as Cleopatra had brought, gifts of clothes and baggage, cattle and money and corn for the exhausted army, and also something Cleopatra had not been able to supply: 2,000 picked soldiers, splendidly armed. Some time ago Octavia had reached Athens with all this, and there received a letter from Antony bidding her await further orders. She had been waiting for weeks, and now wrote to ask what she was to do with her gifts.

Up to now, Octavia had been to Cleopatra simply a political rival, standing in the way of her design to detach Antony from the western Roman world and attach him firmly to her own ambitions.

This letter was clearly that rival's bid to get him back to the Roman side.

"And to *her* side!" thought Cleopatra, suddenly aware of the first pang of a very unpleasant, and to her, not very familiar sensation.

"Careful, careful," she told herself as she recognised it for what it was, "don't let *that* get a hold on you! Personal hatred doesn't mix well with politics."

But this was a generalisation, a moral maxim harder to apply than she imagined: one which she had, until now, not needed to apply.

Her hatred of her sister Arsinoe and of her two brothers had been as nearly impersonal as hatred can be, founded on a healthy realisation of *their* implacable enmity. It had been a case of "kill or be killed". This was quite a different emotion, she was to find, impossible to gratify by the ruthlessness she had used in that life and death struggle.

The elimination of Octavia, as a piece in a political game, was still vital. But it was not enough. Octavia must be cut out of Antony's heart. And at all costs, she must be stopped from joining him again. He pretended to ridicule his "Roman wife" as a prig and a bluestocking. The fact remained that the bluestocking had held him away from Cleopatra for three years, and borne him three children. So the snowflake was capable of melting! Antony was weak. The woman who happened to be *there* was the woman who ruled his heart—so long as she was there. Like water in your hands was this man. But water could so easily slip through the fingers!

Cleopatra had arrived out here still in the weak and emotional condition that so often follows childbirth. This unexpected attack of jealousy still further upset her balance. For some weeks she was really ill, went very thin and languid, and often burst into fits of weeping.

She tried at first to control herself, fearing to alienate Antony just when she desired most strongly to captivate him. But to her surprise her weakness seemed actually to increase his affection. Probably it brought out that same protective, paternal side of his nature which had won him the adoration of his men.

Observing this, she cunningly made use of it. She still pretended to try and control her tears, but made sure he saw them first, then turned away, ostentatiously drying her eyes. Whenever he had to leave her, she held on to his hand beseechingly. Whenever he came back she greeted him with almost swooning rapture.

This was a new Cleopatra, and it seemed to go down well with Antony, who took it all at face value.

The ultimate result was a double victory for Cleopatra, personal and political. Octavia's reinforcements and supplies were accepted : that was a military necessity. But Octavia herself was sent back to Rome.

"Neither she, nor any other woman, shall ever come between us again," vowed Antony. "I'm yours, every inch of me. Nothing shall ever part us, not even death. When I die, I want to be buried by your side, in Alexandria."

Cleopatra had begun with the intent to use the General for her own political purposes. She had gone on to find pleasure in him as a man. Now, for the first time, she began to love him; not as a queen might, for the use she could make of him, but like any woman might love the man in whom she found such joy.

11 *An Egyptian Dream*

IN fact, Antony and Cleopatra were to be parted for a good deal of the eighteen months that followed, in body, though not in spirit.

Antony's forces all had to be reorganised and re-equipped, and new military plans worked out. When this was done, he finally marched in the following spring into Armenia again. This time he conquered it and took captive King Artavasdes, who had so quickly deserted when things went against the Romans, and so brought about the main disaster.

Antony did not meddle with the Parthians this time. They had quarrelled with the King of Media (apparently over the booty captured from the Roman army in its retreat), and seemed unlikely to cause fresh trouble for the time being. So Antony contented himself with an alliance with the King of Media. As a symbol of this, a little Median Princess was betrothed to Anthony's six-year-old son Alexander Helios.

He then went back to Alexandria to celebrate the success with an official "Triumph", Roman-style, the first of its kind to be seen in Egypt.

This was followed by a pageant, staged in the spacious grounds of the gymnasium before Egyptian notables and as many of the Greek and Egyptian citizens of Alexandria as could cram themselves in. Ancient triumph songs from the times of the great Pharaohs were unearthed by the priests, rewritten to suit modern tastes, and declaimed to music by some of the foremost musicians.

Cleopatra was dressed as usual for such public occasions, to represent the goddess Isis. Antony was dressed as himself, in his scarlet general's cloak and Roman tunic, his broad-bladed "Hercules" sword belted low on the hips.

Six-year old Alexander Helios, being now engaged to a princess of Media, wore the Median costume, with a tall peaked cap. His sister wore a charming copy of an ancient Egyptian princess's coronet, like a wreath of forget-me-nots. The youngest little boy, only just able to walk, called Ptolemy Philadelphus after his mother's family, went staggering about the platform in a pair of little boots and a Macedonian cloak and cap.

And Caesarion, now thirteen, wore the traditional Pharaoh's stiff apron and tall starched cap surmounted by the sacred cobra.

Cleopatra frowned a little whenever her eyes fell on her eldest son. With his gangling arms and legs and protruding ears and teeth, he looked uncannily like his dead uncle Ptolemy at the same age. She tried to be patient, reminding herself of Julius Caesar's surprising compassion towards that hated brother.

"He'll fill out in time," she kept telling herself. But would the boy's *brains* fill out? That was the question.

Well, she must do all she could to train him to meet his destiny. For from this day, Ptolemy Caesar was to be her co-ruler. Jointly they were proclaimed "Queen of Kings" and "King of Kings": Joint Pharaohs of the Two Lands of Egypt, and of Cyprus.

There was a fanfare of the strange, old, throaty-sounding trumpets of Egypt, and a soft susurration of sistrums, like a multitude of small birds taking flight. And then the long, long list of titles customary for all rulers of Egypt was intoned before the crowds.

After this the younger children were installed: Alexander as the King of Armenia, Media and Parthia (though that last kingdom was, strictly speaking, still not within Antony's power to bestow!); little Cleopatra as the Queen of Libya and Cyren-

aica; and baby Ptolemy Philadelphus as King of Syria and
Cilicia.

The people cheered loud and long. They had enjoyed the
pageantry, and had no particular objection to these infants
taking over their various domains. The Egyptians amongst them
had only the haziest idea of the exact location of the foreign
lands being distributed in this lordly way. For though Alexandria was the most cosmopolitan of cities, the Egyptians themselves were great stay-at-homes.

Still, they loved to see a family of pretty children, and were
whole-hearted in their approval of their queen and her brood of
little monarchs. As for Antony, he was something of a minor
attraction, though popular enough. The citizens of Alexandria
had not yet forgotten how he once begged for their lives, when
the hated "flute player", father of Cleopatra, on regaining his
throne by Roman arms, had wanted wholesale executions.

In his speech on this occasion of "the Donations" as they
called the pageant, Antony carefully avoided claiming any royal
title for himself. All these arrangements, he declared, were made
by virtue of his authority as one of the Roman Triumvirs, and
in memory of Julius Caesar, who had been the previous
husband of their queen, and whose son was the legitimate heir.

But in fact, if not in name, he had now become Cleopatra's
king-consort. As such he would probably have been content to
settle down in Egypt to rule with her over "our half-world" as
he called it, if Octavian had been content to leave him alone.

Cleopatra had no illusions on that score. She had far too
much intelligence not to see what a flimsy house of cards her
family of kings and queens would be without the armies to keep
it up.

"Octavian is only waiting until he's strong enough to attack
you," she constantly warned Antony. "We ought to attack *him*
before he's ready."

But Antony shrank from outright civil war; he hankered still
for a peaceful co-existence with his rival.

"I still have many friends in the Roman Senate," he

declared. "Sosius, and my old co-campaigner Ahenobarbus are to be Consuls next year. They'll do something for me, I have no doubt."

"Don't be so sure!" retorted Cleopatra. "As for Ahenobarbus, he's no friend of mine, whatever he may be to you. And what can he do against a man like Octavian? Octavian is sly, and also utterly ruthless. He's busy even now, quietly blackening your name and mine. Do you know that I am said to be a drunkard, a poisoner, a traitor and a coward? I worship beasts. I am an eastern whore. Caesarion is a bastard. I am a sorceress who has bewitched you, drugged you into a state of degenerate lust, and will drag you to your ruin! That's the kind of lie he's spreading about! And this damages *you*. The mud splashes off on *you*, don't you see, my darling?

"Octavia's conduct isn't doing you any good either. 'Such a *good* woman' they say, 'to be treated so abominably by Mark Antony!'"

"We have to admit that she is behaving very creditably," said Antony somewhat tactlessly, "looking after not only her own children, but Fulvia's also, and doing her utmost to soften her brother towards me, and keep him from any act of violence."

"That's all for effect! It only turns people the more against you, as she very well knows."

Cleopatra had never been able to rid herself of her poisonous jealousy of Octavia. It warped her political judgment to some extent, and through her, Antony's. Consequently he made the mistake of sending Octavia letters of formal divorce, and an order to leave his house in Rome. It was an act of useless provocation. On the one hand, he had no intention of rejoining Octavia, and regarded his marriage to Cleopatra as entirely legitimate. On the other hand in the eyes of orthodox Romans the action made no improvement to his position. For to them, divorced or not, he could never legally be married to a foreigner.

Meanwhile, plenty more had been added to the score on both sides.

One day Octavian went to the temple of the Vestal Virgins, supposed to be sacred territory, forcibly took away Antony's will, and caused it to be read aloud in the Senate.

Many Senators were scandalised to hear that Cleopatra's son Caesarion was declared by Antony to be Caesar's legitimate heir: and still more scandalised that Antony, a Roman, should leave his property to his own children by this "Egyptian whore", and even ask that his body be buried with hers in Alexandria. Others were equally shocked by Octavian's action. He had no right, they said, to read out a man's will before his death, let alone snatch it out of the sacred hands of the Vestal Virgins.

Tension mounted.

Antony wrote to his friends in the Senate, asking it to ratify his arrangements at the "Donations" in Alexandria, and making three demands: first, the four legions Octavian had promised him seven years ago; second, the right of recruiting soldiers in Italy: and third, some Italian land on which to settle his retired soldiers.

He also reproached Octavian for not sharing Sicily, lately taken from the pirate Sextus Pompeius, and for not returning the hundred and twenty ships Antony lent him for that purpose.

Octavian's answers were not merely unsatisfactory. They were downright insulting. He would share Sicily with Antony, he said, if Antony was willing to share Armenia. Antony's veterans could settle in Media and Parthia which, he sneered, "their brave actions had added to the Roman domains". There was no mention of the four missing legions. But at last seventy of the hundred and twenty borrowed ships were returned to Alexandria, in not too good a shape.

"This is sheer insolence! Almost a declaration of war!" said Antony.

"Octavian won't trouble to *declare* war. He's been *making* war for the last two years at least, without any warning," Cleopatra told him scornfully.

It was clear enough that the storm was gathering in earnest.

Antony's two friendly Consuls tried to bring in a vote of censure against Octavian, but failed, blocked by the veto of a tribune. All over Italy cities were taking oaths of allegiance to Octavian as their personal leader, despite the crushing taxes he was imposing.

The two Consuls, with nearly four hundred senators, left Rome and came to join Antony.

It seemed to both sides that their following and resources were about equally balanced. It was only a question of the right moment to begin the war.

CLEOPATRA'S attitude to the Parthian campaign had been one of reluctant loyalty. But into the war against Octavian she threw her whole heart, and every kind of help at her command.

She undertook to pay and feed the whole of Antony's forces, and for a start, placed in their common war chest a sum of 20,000 talents. She also contributed to the joint navy a squadron of sixty warships and a hundred and fifty transport ships, as well as a large number of oarsmen. These she personally accompanied to Ephesus, where Antony was spending the winter, gathering his men from Armenia and his ships from all over the eastern seas, and extracting oaths of allegiance from the puppet-kings he had set up in Syria and Asia Minor.

As the winter went by, it began to be clear to her that her presence in Ephesus was not precisely welcome to Antony's Roman officers, nor even to Antony himself. In fact, one day, in the presence of several of the officers (probably drawing courage from their presence) he told her outright that it might be better if she were now to retire to Egypt, leaving the actual conduct of this war to himself.

Greatly to her surprise, one of the officers, called Canidius, spoke up vigorously on her behalf.

"Sir!" he pointed out to Antony. "We have to admit that the

Queen of Egypt is paying handsomely towards this campaign. She who pays the piper ought to have some say in the tune, I think. Moreover, in my opinion the queen is in no way inferior in good sense to any of these kings we have serving with us, in fact much *more* sensible than most of 'em. After all, she's kept her crown on her head these—what is it—fifteen years? No small achievement these days, when kings go down like skittles. As for the actual details of war strategy, I'm sure she has the sense to keep her nose out of all that. Though if she weren't a woman, by Hercules, I reckon there's the makings of a general in her."

There were some sly grins and a few guffaws at this speech, but for the time being no more talk of her going home to Egypt.

The Roman officers were not the only ones who had been urging Antony to get rid of Cleopatra. A short time before, Herod of Judaea, whom she had at one time befriended, but then antagonised by her ruthless bargaining, had privately come to him with a piece of brutal advice.

"Murder the woman," he had said, "and annex Egypt! Otherwise I can't see much future for you. They'll never stomach a foreign queen in Rome, especially a woman they look on as a whore, if you'll pardon the expression."

"She happens to be my wife!" Antony reminded him, with a dangerous glint in his eye.

"Yes, yes, but as I said, in *their* eyes . . . !"

Herod grimaced.

It was typical of Herod, such advice: thoroughly cold-blooded and cynical. And of course quite unthinkable. Kill his Egyptian love, the very pulse of his heart, and the mother of his children? Who but a monster could even dream of such a deed?

But the fellow *had* something, all the same. It was perfectly true that, short of murder, there was no way at all of shaking off this woman, at once so embarrassing to his cause and so vital to it.

Well, so what! He would win through yet. If the Romans,

the Herods and the rest didn't like her, they'd have to lump it! And the common men, *his* men, surely they would follow wherever he chose to lead? They always had. They would again, Cleopatra or no Cleopatra.

He had a land army of nineteen legions, all Italians, well seasoned troops, plus about 10,000 light-armed Asiatics, and 12,000 cavalry. He had, with Cleopatra's ships, eight squadrons, fine ships many of them, strongly bound with iron against ramming, with the maximum banks of oars. Octavian would be hard put to match all this. Antony shook off his doubts and went on with his preparations. In the spring he moved his forces to the island of Samos. Here, while the transport ships ferried the legions across to Athens, the priests of Dionysus put on performances of religious plays, and offered sacrifices, by way of a blessing on the war. With typical extravagance, Antony in return presented them with the whole town of Pirene.

A month later Antony and Cleopatra were both loudly welcomed by the citizens of Athens. But even here, where Antony was so popular, discontent against Cleopatra was persistent amongst the Romans. There were daily desertions from the army; and two senators who had bitterly opposed Cleopatra's part in the war, left for Rome at this time, taking inside knowledge of Antony's plans to Octavian.

It was in Athens, too, that there came a message from Antony's friends in Rome, saying all would go well if he would only send the Queen of Egypt packing. Perhaps from a secret uneasiness, Antony treated the messenger with the most reckless insolence, and finally threw him out of doors.

By the autumn everything was ready. Antony's plans were made, and his forces disposed all along the east coast of the Ionian Sea, from the south of Greece northwards to the island of Corcyra, the largest force in the Actium peninsula, which was strongly fortified. Headquarters were at Patrae, just west of the gulf of Corinth.

And here they waited.

"But why?" Cleopatra demanded. "Why not strike now, before Octavian has time to finish his preparations? Why not sail across to Italy at once and attack him in his own territory?"

He had to tell her at last outright:

"Because I can't trust my men to fight in Italy."

"Because of me?"

"I'm afraid so."

"So you wish me to leave you?"

Cleopatra's great eyes blazed out unmistakably the answer she was demanding. And he hastily made it.

"No, no! Of course not! What should I do without you? Besides," he laughed impudently, which was the only way he knew how to stand up to her, "As you well know, where my heart is, there is my treasure chest also!"

"No, but seriously," he went on hurriedly before she might take offence at this blunt realism, "you must see that in the circumstances I have no choice but to wait here, hoping to draw the enemy across to me."

Octavian was not to be drawn that autumn, though he did at last formally declare "a just war" as he called it, not upon Antony, but upon Cleopatra alone.

"Typical Octavian cunning!" commented Antony. "He knows I have so many friends in Italy that he'd never get enough support against me."

"Charmion, why do they hate me so much?" marvelled Cleopatra. "What has Egypt done to earn such hatred?"

"Nothing that I know of, my lady. But we felt it all round us in Rome. Remember?"

"Yes, I remember."

"Oh, my lady! If only we were back in Egypt where everybody loves you!" burst out Charmion. "I sometimes wish—forgive me for saying it—that you'd never meddled with these Romans!"

"I had no choice. Don't you see, if I'd just sat waiting in Egypt, after Caesar's death, sooner or later Rome would have meddled with us? And that would have meant the end of

Egypt. This way at least there's an equal chance of utter ruin, or glory. Do you remember, Charmion, that Greek prophet who once came to the palace?"

"The one who foretold that Egypt was to cast Rome down, and then begin a Golden Age, with Asia and Europe united in brotherly love and war banished from the earth! I should think so!" said Charmion, sceptically.

"I don't know, Charmion. It's possible these prophets know things that we don't. Sometimes I've wondered if that could be my destiny. Just imagine, Charmion, if I, and Antony of course, should succeed where even Alexander failed! East and West, one peaceful world! And Egypt the centre of it!"

12 A Forlorn Hope

NOT until the spring of the following year, when Cleopatra had begun to look with some dismay into her much-depleted war-chest, were Octavian and his fleet at length reported to have set sail from Italy.

"Meet him! Meet him at sea!" urged Cleopatra. "We have five hundred ships to his four hundred."

But Antony did not agree.

"I must draw him here to fight on land. I'm his match on land," was his contention. "But at sea he has his old friend Agrippa in command. Octavian would never be where he is now if it hadn't been for Agrippa. Not to mention Agrippa's new catapults."

So Octavian was allowed to land his army and take up a position on high ground across the water from the Actium peninsula, where Antony's men were encamped. This position he quickly fortified, so strongly that all through that summer Antony tried in vain either to take it or to tempt him out of it.

Meanwhile Agrippa, with most of Octavian's fleet, sailed further south and, one by one, took possession of all those points which Antony had so carefully fortified the previous winter: bases from which it was easy to attack Egyptian ships bringing corn for the forces. Agrippa also took Antony's headquarters near Corinth, and Corinth itself. This meant that corn could not be brought by the alternative route, by sea east of Greece, and then across the Isthmus of Corinth.

By August things were desperate. Antony's forces were

virtually besieged. The men were suffering from all kinds of diseases. Rations were short. Corn had to be carried on men's backs across the mountains, extracted first from the country people by force. Puppet-kings and even Roman officers were deserting in shoals. Antony tried to stop that by executions, but it merely increased the rot.

Towards the end of August Antony called a council of war, which Cleopatra insisted upon attending. There were some dirty looks at her, but she resolutely ignored them. Not only their future, but their very lives, depended upon the decisions of the next few days. She was not going to be driven out of her proper share of those decisions.

She had urged Antony at the very beginning to meet Octavian's forces before they ever touched land. The war could well have been won by now if her advice had been followed. And even if lost, could their plight be any worse than it was?

She had more sense than to say so in public. But she did urge, with all the power at her command, that the fleet ought to be used now.

"It's our only chance!" she cried, in her low, vibrant voice. "And it's still a good chance. We still have four hundred ships left, fine, modern ships too. We must fight our way out! Or there'll soon be not a man left of your legions, what with famine, disease and desertion."

Canidius, who had once been her friend, had now changed sides.

"Fine ships, madam, are no use without the men to sail them. No, sir!" he turned his back on her and spoke to Antony alone. "Let the Queen retire to Egypt, with her own squadron of ships if she pleases! Let *us* retreat with what's left of the army, into Macedonia. We can recruit fresh men there. You know that ground well. And on land, Mark Antony, nobody can match you. You were never a naval commander, sir! It's madness to chop up your disciplined army into little bits, and parcel them out into ships, when you know so much better how to lay them out on land."

There was a general hum of agreement. And an elderly infantry officer, face and body gnarled and twisted with long service, cried out :

"Ay, general! Have you forgotten our wounds and our swords, that you put your trust in rotten timbers? Let Egyptians and Phoenicians fight it out at sea. Give us Romans the land where we know how to die or conquer!"

The hum burst into a roar. Cleopatra, in terror lest all should give way to this emotionalism, hurriedly broke in :

"But the army has already done everything possible to break through, and failed! How will you get your men into Macedonia, with Octavian sitting where he has sat for the last six months? And if you do somehow break through, but lose the battle, how will the remnants get back to their homes without the ships you want to abandon here? And may I point out that at least one hundred of those ships are mine? I think I have some right to say whether they are to be abandoned or not?"

She did not speak it, knowing well by now the antagonism under all those cropped and grizzled pates. But she thought : "Even if the battle at sea were lost there would be some hope of getting back to Egypt. All is not lost while we still have Egypt."

To her intense relief and surprise, against almost every man present, Antony agreed with her. And of course, as supreme commander, his was the last word.

On that coast in the summer season the wind usually blows lightly from the sea during the morning. But about midday it turns round, blowing strongly from the north-west.

"We'll make use of that wind," said Antony. "We'll keep them waiting and guessing all the morning. When the wind shifts, we'll try to turn their left flank. If we manage that, we'll hoist sails and drive them down-wind, away from their camp."

It sounded an excellent plan, and was generally approved.

Afterwards however, alone with Cleopatra and Canidius, Antony proposed a second plan in case the first one failed.

In that case he and Cleopatra were to break through and sail for Egypt with what ships they had, while Canidius, with the remainder of the troops left on land, was to get them back as best he could via Macedonia.

Canidius received this second plan with glum looks. Observing which, Antony cried:

"One has to remember the *possibility* of defeat and plan for it. But we shall win, man. Never fear, Canidius, we shall win!"

But there was something in the way he spoke that sent a small shiver across Cleopatra's scalp.

"He's afraid we shall lose," she said to herself. And privately she gave orders for the war chest to be shipped aboard one of her own Egyptian transports. In case of defeat that money would come in very useful. In case of victory, well, it would come to no harm!

But the shipmasters and the troops drew their own, too simple, conclusions from this act.

The shipping of the sails also gave rise to much dismay. It was unusual in a sea battle to take the sails on board. Oars were so much more manoeuvrable in a close fight. As Antony's second plan was not generally made public, it was not unnaturally concluded he meant to run before the enemy, rather than to fight. But this Antony did not realise until much later.

AFTER three days of storms the sky was clear again, and sea and air more or less at rest.

Outside the peninsula the water was even yet quite choppy. The Egyptian flagship, the *Antonias*, was bobbing like a great duck as Cleopatra paced the deck, and a lively breeze tugged at her hair.

But it had been judged to be calm enough for the great attack. And ever since daybreak the air had been all alive with the hoarse cries of crews and shipmasters, and the coxswains' drums, and the splash and creak of oars, as the great warships, like huge marine centipedes, slipped one by one from the harbour and out to the open sea.

The deploying of four hundred of these monsters into ordered line was no easy operation. But it had been conducted with minimum confusion, in excellent discipline, which augured well for the coming battle.

Now, shortly before midday, all were drawn up in their places, spread-eagled across the wide entrance to the bay, six squadrons of them in one great shallow crescent, the single Egyptian squadron in a smaller crescent behind the centre.

The ships on the horns of the larger crescent were so far away that they looked as small as water-boatmen on a stagnant pond. But the air was clear after the storms, and Cleopatra's sight was keen. She could make out quite easily the white pennon flying from the mast of Antony's flagship on the northernmost tip of the crescent. From the *Antonias'* high deck she could also see quite distinctly the enemy ships, spread out in a long matching crescent, a mile further out to sea.

Under the high noon sun the ships lay still, or as nearly so as ships can ever be. Half a million oars hung over the water, waiting only for the signal to plunge in as one. Along the *Antonias'* sides the water softly clucked. A few seabirds wailed on the distant cliffs. It was so quiet, she felt she could have whispered to Antony across the mile of water.

"How beautiful!" she wanted to cry out.

It was the first time she had ever seen a fleet of ships drawn up for battle. She had been taught by Intef, Egyptian-wise, to regard all warfare, by sea or land, as an unpleasant though often unavoidable means to a political end. Now for the first time she understood how it could be for some men an exhilaration, a joy even, sought for its own sake.

"Wind's dropped!" said the Master of the *Antonias*. "Reckon we haven't long to wait now."

Following his pointing finger she saw that the *Antonias'* pennon, which had been flickering shorewards all the morning, hung limp as an oarsman's sweat-rag.

They stood waiting, their eyes on the pennon.

The sun's disc burned down like a great gong of vibrating

brass. The light breastplate Cleopatra wore as a precaution
against stray arrows was so hot that she had to hold her arms
away from her body. Between the motionless oars the water
winked like myriads of emerald eyes. . . .

"She's here! See!" exclaimed the captain, pointing. And she
saw that the pennon was stirring, lifting, feebly but unmistakably towards the south.

"*Ha-a-a-a-h!*"

The sound travelled slowly along the crescent of ships, in a
long crescendo like a breaking wave, as a thousand pairs of
watching eyes registered the same signal.

A second sound came chasing after it, in a gravelly roar: the
roll of the coxswains' drums. And all that multitude of oars
clapped hands together with the water.

"Right! Coxswain, begin!" cried the captain.

At which all other noises were drowned in the beat of the
Antonias' drum, and the rhythmic groan and splash of all her
oars.

With a majestic lift of her great prow, the flagship swung
away northwards and out to sea—not too fast, keeping pace
with the general movement forward.

It all looked so orderly, so utterly natural, that there seemed
no reason to doubt that the operation must succeed.

From the *Antonias* it was possible to see that Antony's squadron and the ships at the corresponding tip of the enemy line
had met, as Antony planned, and engaged in battle. The details
of the struggle were impossible to make out, though the look-out
man on the mast reported a great deal of hard fighting. After
some time, Antony's flagship was seen to be in desperate com-
bat, grappled by one of the enemy, and in great danger of being
sunk.

Cleopatra ached to sail her own squadron to his rescue. But
her orders had been quite definite: to keep behind the middle
two of the Roman squadrons: later, to close up the gap which
would be left when these moved round to follow Antony's ships

in turning the flank of the enemy. She was much too inexperienced in naval matters to risk disobeying these orders.

Yet it proved impossible to carry them out. Before the struggle on the right had come to a clear decision, the whole of the left of the front line, three squadrons, had backed water and were rowing like mad back to the harbour!

The central two squadrons would have deserted in the same fashion if Cleopatra's ships had not stood in the way. They solved their problem very simply. Rapidly, ship by ship, almost as if to numbers, their oars rose vertically into the air, in token of submission to the enemy.

"We can't leave one squadron to cope with the whole of the enemy! We must go to Mark Antony's help, whatever his orders!" Cleopatra was urging the Master, when, to her intense relief (for, complete novice though she was, she could see very well that the whole battle was already lost) there fluttered up on the mast of Antony's ship the red pennon which was the prearranged signal for her own retreat.

"Hoist sails! Hoist sails!" cried the Master.

And quickly, one after another, sixty sails rose quivering into the air, and turned and filled.

The wind blew steadily. In a very few hours the Egyptian ships were out of sight of the enemy, well down the coast of Greece, where in a day or so they were joined by what was left of Antony's squadron, and by Antony himself.

FOR three days after he came aboard the Egyptian flagship, Antony would speak to no one. He sat alone at the prow, refusing all food, his shoulders humped, his chin in his hands, his eyes on the ever receding horizon, beyond which lay his defeat and his disgrace.

"Mark Antony is at his best in misfortune": that was what people had always said of this man. Over and over again his men had extolled his marvellous courage and resource throughout the disastrous retreat from the Parthians. Yet here he was, behaving as if this latest set-back were the final irretrievable ruin.

Cleopatra refused to believe it.

"You still have your forty ships. We have our sixty," she pleaded with him. "Canidius may yet bring the remains of the army through to Egypt. You have four legions in North Africa, and eleven altogether in Syria and Macedonia and Egypt. The treasure chest is intact. Octavian can't make war everywhere at once. And between us we still have some formidable reserves."

She managed at last to rouse him to some extent. He made an effort at least to emerge from complete collapse, and presently, leaving her to go back with her squadron to Alexandria, he took his own ships to see what he could do in North Africa.

Cleopatra came home in style, with the garlands of victory at her mast. The lie would soon be discovered of course. But it gave her time to make sure of her position, and to execute one or two potential rebels. There were few of these. It was the end of the month of Thoth. The floods had arrived, satisfactorily abundant. Victorious or not in the foreign lands, her people were fairly indifferent, so long as she had played her part in ensuring the harvest.

"Perhaps we may yet come through!" she persuaded herself in the first few weeks.

But no sooner had Antony reached North Africa than his four legions deserted to Octavian's commander. And presently Canidius came to Alexandria, a refugee in danger of his life, without a single man out of the army they had left with him. In less than seven days after the fiasco at Actium, he reported, they had all gone over to Octavian.

"I'm finished!" said Antony when, on his return, he was confronted with this news. "I'm a ruined man! Ruined for your sake!" he bitterly told Cleopatra.

"I could just as well claim that I have ruined myself for *your* sake!" retorted Cleopatra. "But I don't. Neither of us is ruined, or need be, if we keep our heads. There's still Egypt, after all. So long as I have Egypt, it is yours too!"

"But you will keep Egypt only as long as Octavian pleases," Antony brutally reminded her. "There isn't a hope of defending it. There isn't a man left in the whole world that I could trust to follow me! Not a single man!"

Nothing Cleopatra could do or say would rouse Antony from utter despair.

She was still full of ideas. Even if Egypt fell, which she could hardly imagine, there were other places in the world. They could sail away to Spain, seize the silver mines, and build up a new kingdom there.

"Not if Octavian knows of it!" jeered Antony.

India then! Octavian had no foot at all in India. They would take the Egyptian ships across to the Red Sea and sail to India, and build there the kingdom which Alexander the Great had failed to sustain.

But Antony had had enough of kingdom building. Instead, he built himself a sort of hermitage out on the end of a specially constructed breakwater near the Pharos. His "Timonium" he called it. He saw himself as a greatly wronged man, betrayed, like the notorious misanthropic Timon of Athens, by all he had imagined to be his friends. There was always something of the play-actor in Antony. But his despair was genuine enough to keep him to this role throughout the winter. Not even Cleopatra was allowed into his hermitage.

In her palace, not very far across the harbour, she was facing the situation alone, in her own way. For a time she persisted in her plan of a flight to India. She even had a number of galleys dragged across to the shore of the Red Sea. But the Arabian king whose bitumen fields had been commandeered for her by Antony, came and burnt the ships, and she had to give up this idea.

For the first time she seriously began to consider the possibility of complete defeat.

Not that even yet she accepted this as unavoidable. It was

true that Antony was now a broken reed. She had backed the wrong man. But what choice had she had? Fate had led her into the association with him, rather than with the one who now seemed certain to be triumphant.

But what of that? Octavian, after all, was a man like any other. She was older now of course, and Octavian was a good deal younger than Antony. But she had never been, strictly speaking, a beautiful woman. Nor had she even relied on youthfulness for her charm. She had always had to make the most of herself, and at thirty-eight she ought to know rather more of the job than at twenty. If she could only get within striking distance of Octavian, there might still be hope for Egypt.

"And if not, Charmion, if I fail," she told her friend and confidante, "I shall take good care not to fall into *his* hands. The Queen of Egypt shall never be seen in a Roman Triumph. That I swear!"

Cleopatra had never forgotten the spectacle of her sister walking in chains along the streets of Rome, amongst hundreds of other wretched prisoners of war, the mob howling in derision as they looked on.

"He will have you guarded closely for precisely that purpose if you are defeated and caught alive."

"I shall not be caught—*alive*!"

"Oh, my lady!" protested Charmion in a horrified whisper, knowing her mistress spoke in deadly earnest.

"The thing is," mused Cleopatra, "the best way. For I'm not very brave about pain. Death is nothing. But pain is a terrible thing to inflict upon oneself in cold blood. I must make some investigations."

Summoning her personal physician, Olympus, she questioned him, in strictest secrecy, not even Charmion being present, as to the detailed effects of all poisons known to him. It seemed all were unsatisfactory. If they were swift they were extremely painful. If fairly painless they were slow, with the consequent danger of discovery before their work was done. There was a long silence.

"My old friend Intef used to tell me," said Cleopatra at last, "that the ancient Pharaohs, when the time came to step down for a younger man, made use of a snake called an asp. What is the effect of the bite of an asp?"

Olympus could not be certain, never having witnessed such a death.

"But," he ventured, "from the appearance of their bodies after death, I should think there was no excessive degree of suffering."

"Is there a criminal in the prisons due for execution?" asked Cleopatra after a moment's thought.

It appeared there were several.

"Arrange for one of them to die in this manner, in my presence," she ordered.

It was not pleasant, of course, to sit and watch a man dying. But she *must* know just what she faced if the worst happened. As for the man, he had to die in any case. He was a murderer. As she silently watched, it seemed fairly certain that this was an easier death than he could have reasonably expected. She could not detect any sign of great suffering. Fear, at the start, of course. But after the actual bite, he merely sank without convulsions or groans, and fairly rapidly, into a drowsy lethargy, and finally into unconsciousness.

She gave orders that henceforth Olympus must have several of these death-bringers conveniently, but discreetly, to hand.

She also began to build a tomb: not in any morbid state of mind, but because each ruler of Egypt customarily prepared his "eternal abode" well in advance. One dwelt in this abode so much longer than in an earthly house: it was therefore worthy of the most lavish care. One needed stone for an eternal tomb, whereas a mud hut was good enough merely to live in on earth. That was the old Egyptian way of looking at things.

The Royal finances would not stretch to a pyramid these days. Cleopatra's tomb had to be fairly modest: a small tower in the palace grounds, near the temple of the Goddess Isis, a tower that could serve if necessary as a tiny fortress, having only one small door and one small window.

To the vaults of this mausoleum she began to transfer her personal treasure, her gold and silver jewellery, her emeralds and pearls and stocks of ebony and ivory. With this was stored a quantity of firewood and tow. If the worst happened she would retreat here, kill herself and set fire to the treasure. Octavian was not going to lay hands on that, any more than he should cause her to walk in his Triumph.

It might never come to that, of course. She was giving other more hopeful orders too : having the frontier towns (Pelusium in the East and Paraetonium in the West) fortified and garrisoned with Egyptian troops. Even these precautions might not be necessary. Octavian was presently reported to have been recalled to Rome, where there were fresh disturbances. He would not leave Rome again before the spring. Perhaps by then he might even decide to leave Antony (that sleeping dog) alone.

Halfway through the winter, tired at last of playing Timon of Athens, Antony left his hermitage and came back to the palace. They were more or less reconciled. Things were not the same, of course. He still loved her as passionately as ever; there was no doubt of that. But there was a new bitterness in him too, which caused him to lash out savagely every now and then. Sometimes he shouted :

"I've ruined my life for your sake! Might as well enjoy what I've paid so dearly for while there's still time !"

Cleopatra's own feelings also were painfully mixed. As an ally Antony had utterly failed her. But after all he was still her husband and the father of three of her children. Whatever his faults, he had been loyal to her and to her cause. She could not desert him now.

Antony did not know, but while he sulked in the Timonium, letters had come from Octavian offering her "every reasonable favour", if she would have Antony put to death.

This was out of the question. She had had her sister done to death without a qualm. Arsinoe had, after all, been her declared enemy, and would have done the same to her given the chance. But Antony—her husband, her proved friend, the sharer of her bed and the father of her family?

No. If this was Octavian's price, it could not be paid. She could not do it, not even for the sake of Egypt.

13　A Roman Death

IT was almost a relief when, with the returning spring, came news that Octavian was on the march in Syria, aiming presumably at Egypt. His second-in-command had meanwhile been sent to attack by the western approach.

Now that there was something definite to face, Antony seemed to recover some of his old spirit. He was still convinced that he was doomed. The odds were massively in Octavian's favour. In numbers Antony was hopelessly outdone, and even the few men left to him were not to be trusted. But at least he would be able to make a fight for it, at the worst, die fighting. Busily occupied in the equipment and exercise of his troops, there were odd moments when he was even able to pretend to himself that by some miracle all might yet be right.

Octavian took his time in coming to grips, and Antony was quite unable to hasten the crisis. There simply were not the men to march out and attack, scarcely enough indeed for the sketchiest defence.

When Paraetonium was occupied by Gallus, Octavian's second-in-command, Antony did what he could to protect Egypt. He lacked the means to contest the city by land. But he still had his forty ships, and with these he sailed to try to recapture the city by sea.

But sea warfare was never his strong line. The ships were poorly manned and the men half-hearted. Antony himself fought with a heavy heart in expectation of defeat. He lost most of his ships and achieved nothing.

After this disaster Antony wrote privately to Octavian, offering to commit suicide if Octavian would spare Cleopatra. The offer was ignored.

"As I might have expected," said Antony later. "He knows he has us both in the hollow of his hand!" It was not in Antony's nature to keep quiet about the heroic self-sacrifice he had offered for Cleopatra's sake.

"You would have done me no good by your death; in fact much ill!" Cleopatra told him sharply, half moved by this evidence of his devotion, but disturbed by a guilty awareness of her own inability to match it.

She loved him still. She had been loyal to him, to the extent of refusing to betray him to their enemy. But actually to give up her life for him was a thing that would never have entered her head. But then, she told herself, how could she afford such gestures? She was more than Cleopatra. She was Egypt also. How best to save Egypt was still her first concern. Romantic heroism was all very well for Antony. It was not for her.

During Antony's absence she had secretly sent to Octavian a sceptre and a crown (not her best ones of course) and offered submission, if Octavian would install one of her sons in her place. Octavian's public reply had ignored her request, demanding complete and unconditional surrender. But with the public letter had come a secret message, bidding her have no fear: Octavian intended her no personal violence, nor any kind of harm.

What use were such vague assurances from such a man? He was only trying in his sly fashion to drive a wedge between Antony and herself. He should not succeed. Clearly there was no course open for them but to fight on together, even in the face of almost certain defeat.

Towards the end of July (Roman calendar) Octavian reached Pelusium. It fell almost immediately: rumour said, partly through Cleopatra's own treachery. But that was nonsense. What possible motive could she have, she protested, to hasten her own end?

After that it was only a matter of days before Octavian reached the suburbs of Alexandria.

Here Antony met him with a small band of his own cavalry. He was by nature and by long experience at his best with cavalry. In a vigorous sally the enemy horse was routed. Antony, in a mood of reckless exaltation, sped to the palace with the news.

"By Hercules!" he cried, finding Cleopatra at the door, "we shall still give them something to think about!"

He was still in his armour, and bloody from the battle. But he embraced her with kisses and boisterous laughter, to the scandal of all present, but especially of the Romans.

Cleopatra, infected by his mood, extravagantly rewarded one of his officers with a gold breastplate and helmet. (They heard that very same night that the recipient had immediately deserted to the enemy.)

By that time Antony's spirits had sunk to the depths. At supper he drank far too much, and spoke openly of his expectations of honourable death tomorrow. He was not maudlin about this: quite calm and philosophical indeed, but he had the whole company, including Cleopatra, in tears before he had finished.

In the morning his mood had changed again, to the cheerfulness of one going serenely to his execution.

Infantry and cavalry marched out of the city at daybreak, taking their positions on a small hill on the outskirts, from where he could see the Egyptian fleet and what was left of his own, advancing towards Octavian's. No sooner was Antony's fleet within shouting distance than up went all their oars—in token of submission to Octavian! The enemy oars lifted vertically in answering salute. And presently the whole flotilla began to row, in unison, back into the harbour.

"Well—there goes my sea battle," said Antony, without apparent emotion. "No more than I expected."

Expected or not, his spirit finally broke when the cavalry, of all things, was the next to desert him.

He fought on for a time with the infantry, which strangely

enough stood firm. But he fought with no heart. And very quickly he saw that they were defeated. To avert total slaughter he ordered a retreat, then left them to their own devices, and ran wildly through the streets towards the palace, shouting aloud, shameless in his agony, that he was finished, betrayed, ruined for the love of a woman.

News of the final catastrophe had beaten him there. The palace was like an anthill kicked open; servants and officials scurried about, scavenging or salvaging what they could. Cleopatra's apartments were all empty, the great doors swung open.

"Where is the Queen?" Antony kept shouting, without getting any answer, until at last finding Diomede, one of her secretaries, scurrying through a door with an armful of papyrus rolls, he seized him by both arms and forced him to answer.

"Gone to her mausoleum with her personal slaves. And I am to follow as quickly as possible with these state documents."

Diomede struggled desperately to free himself, green to the lips with terror.

"You're lying! She's dead!" said Antony, who had known for some time of Cleopatra's plan of suicide if the worst happened.

"Very likely! I don't know! Let me go, sir, please!" cried Diomede, bursting into tears. Antony released him, convinced by his manner that Cleopatra, if not already dead, would very soon be so.

"What's left for *me* now?" he asked himself grimly. "I only hung on for her sake. And now she's stolen a march on me. But, by Hercules, you shan't be long before me, Cleopatra! It shan't be said that Antony had less courage than a woman."

Wrenching at the fastenings of his breastplate he hurried to his own apartments and drew his sword: aware even as he did so of a certain nausea. Not that he had any real desire to continue his life. But something lurked in his heart that still drew back from death.

"Come man! What Cleopatra could do, *you* can!" he told himself in disgust.

But that hidden feeling must have resisted to the last. When he threw himself upon his sword, it entered not his heart but his stomach.

"Ye gods!" he thought as he fell. "A bungler to the last!"

The pain was frightful, and blood flowed freely, but it was clear that dying would be long drawn out. Groaning and bawling for someone to come and put an end to him, he dragged himself to a couch, lay down and lost consciousness.

When he came to, it was to find Diomede standing over him, blinking and cracking his fingers in the irritating way he had.

"Oh, sir!" cried the secretary reproachfully as Antony opened his eyes. "You shouldn't have done this, sir! It's so upsetting for the poor Queen!"

"The Queen? But you said she was dead."

"Oh, sir! No!—I didn't know what to believe, but I'm sure I never actually said . . . The Queen, in any case, has been told, and has sent me to bring you to her in the monument if you are fit to be moved, sir!"

"Yes, yes! It's all one to me. She shall have her way, to the last," murmured Antony with a gleam of his old humour.

It was a dreadful business getting him into the mausoleum. Lying on the couch, the bleeding had staunched itself. But lifting him on to the stretcher opened the wound again. Cleopatra dared not open the door of her little fortress. So the stretcher had to be hauled up to the high window on ropes by Cleopatra herself and her two women, the only occupants of the refuge. He bled heavily again and was barely conscious when they laid him on Cleopatra's bed.

Tears pouring down her face, hands and breasts smeared with blood from his body, Cleopatra was still her practical self.

"Bring some water, Iras!—and some clean cloths. We must bind up the wound at once. To think that fool of a Diomede hadn't the sense to do it before he was brought here!" she exclaimed.

Antony's eyes opened at this, and a grimace, probably intended for a smile, twitched at his mouth.

"No, my dear. Let me alone. I'm done. Water's no good to me. Let's have some wine. That's all I want. And to die in your arms."

In less than half an hour he was granted both wishes. Cleopatra, who knelt beside the bed with his head in her arms, weeping quietly, stroking his sweaty face and tangled curls, long since turned grey, and murmuring between her tears the foolish things of their love, suddenly felt the full weight of his head, and saw that the colour was draining swiftly from his face.

She slid his shoulders to the bed and rose stiffly to her feet.

"Charmion, and Iras, we shall have to be his mourners. There's no one else," she said.

And so, together, the three women began to perform the ritual without which no dead man might enter upon the long journey to the "Western world". It was a job left as a rule for paid mourners. But they did their best as amateurs, beating and scratching their naked breasts, dishevelling their hair, to the accompaniment of long rhythmical wails. Cleopatra at least made up fully for any lack of professional style, by her passion.

Before they were through, there came knocking at the door below.

"Go down and see who that is, Iras!" said Cleopatra, breaking off to listen, and resuming hurriedly.

Iras returned with a frightened look.

"It's a messenger from Octavian for you. Says his name's Proculeius," she reported.

Cleopatra's wails abruptly ended. This was serious. Proculeius was one of Octavian's most intimate friends: but a man, according to Antony, friendly towards herself.

"Carry on by yourselves," she told her two women, as she went down to him.

She had no intention of letting Proculeius in, of course. They were not going to catch her as easily as that! This tower, with the treasure down in the vaults, was her last and only bargaining point. That, and Octavian's known desire to take her alive, for his Triumph.

So she spoke to the Roman through the grille of the heavily barred ground-floor door.

As she expected, he had come with only the vague assurances that she must trust Octavian to treat her with honour. She in return stuck to her old demand that the kingdom be transferred to one of her sons. Promising to put her case once more to his master, Proculeius departed, and Cleopatra returned to her interrupted mourning.

This was barely over when there came knocking again below.

It was not Proculeius this time but Gallus, the commander who defeated Antony in Africa. But it was the same old story: no ground at all on which she could possibly begin to negotiate.

She told him so, plainly and repeatedly, while he as often put forward the same "nothing" in varying words. They were still at it after a full hour, when suddenly Charmion cried out:

"Oh, my lady! Look behind! We've been tricked!"

Turning sharply, Cleopatra saw Proculeius running down the stairs with the two officers behind him. She whipped out the dagger she now always carried in her belt. But Proculeius was too quick for her. Springing forward he seized both her hands.

"No! Oh no! Why, for shame! Haven't we told you that you have nothing to fear?" he cried reproachfully, and firm but gentle, drew the dagger out of her hand. He even had the impudence to shake her dress, to make sure there was no poison in the folds, he explained, in response to her indignant looks.

"Octavian does not wish for your death!" he repeated.

It was obvious that the game was up. They had tricked her out of her last bolt-hole. As she left the mausoleum with Proculeius and his men, she saw dangling from the upper window the rope ladder by which they had entered while Gallus held her in talk at the door.

14 *The Golden Serpent*

LIKE Antony, Cleopatra now had no wish to go on living, yet hesitated to die. But while he had hesitated only for a few moments, she delayed for nearly a month. Basically more optimistic—and much more stubborn—she still could not bring herself to believe there was no hope left.

During that month she was Octavian's prisoner. He was true to his promise and was certainly treating her with honour. She lived more or less as she was accustomed, in her own royal apartments, with her own staff of slaves, in the style befitting the Queen of Egypt. But she knew very well that she was no longer the real Queen. Dwelling in the palace, unobtrusively the master of all her servants, was Octavian's freedman Epaphroditus, a charming young man, courteous as any woman could wish, yet in fact her jailer.

Octavian himself she saw only once. He came to see her soon after Antony's funeral. She had been allowed to spend as much as she liked (of her own money) on that, and to superintend the arrangements personally. Mark Antony had been buried in a manner appropriate to his greatness (and hers) in the mausoleum she had intended for her own body. She had even been allowed out of the palace for the occasion (under guard of course) to follow the body to the tomb.

Afterwards she was very ill. The ulceration of her breasts, caused by the severe lacerations of her mourning at the death-bed, had brought on a fever. She was refusing all food too, hoping that starvation plus the fever would bring about her own death.

Possibly Octavian knew what was in her mind and came to weigh up for himself the chances of the success of this second attempt at suicide. At any rate, she knew the moment she set eyes on him that she might as well give up for ever the secret hope she had been cherishing, all this time, of adding Octavian to her list of lovers.

Julius Caesar had admired her, respected her, liked her and finally, in his own way, loved her. Mark Antony had adored her. But this man would never be anything but her cool and steely enemy.

There was nothing personal about his enmity. He was courteous, even kind, in his enquiries as to her illness and his entreaties to care for herself better. All those lies about her which he had set drifting across the world were clearly nothing but political propaganda. He believed none of them.

But it was as plain as daylight that she could expect no power over him as a woman. Not that Octavian was not susceptible to women. They said indeed that he had been madly in love with his Livia when he divorced his first wife for her sake. They said he still adored Livia, despite the fact that she had produced him no children, and despite the fact that he had plenty of other women at his command, not to mention a few young boys.

But this was plainly a man who, though he might readily indulge his passions, would never do so to his own disadvantage, or against his own cool judgment.

"Antony was right," she said to Charmion when he had gone. "We're finished. Neither I nor my children will ever rule again in Egypt. The only thing is whether I can still do anything to save at least their lives. Are they safer with me alive or with me dead? What do *you* say?"

Charmion burst into tears. No more than Cleopatra herself could she answer this question.

Cleopatra's four children, and Antony's son Antyllus, were being kept under the same sort of house-arrest as herself, in another part of the palace. She was not able to see them, or they her. During his visit Octavian had assured her once more that he meant them no harm. But there had been something in his look even as he spoke these fair words, which had re-awakened her distrust, particularly as regarded Caesarion. As the son of Julius Caesar, Caesarion could be a possible rival, and a danger to Octavian's hold as master of Rome.

After Octavian's sick-bed visit, she decided to call off her hunger strike, to cling to life at any rate long enough to try to do something for the safety of her eldest son.

Although she could not leave the palace, she had a certain amount of contact with the world outside. Her private physi-cian, Olympus, was allowed to come and go quite freely, and not, she was fairly certain, from any hidden disloyalty to herself. The slaves, especially the garden staff, had to be in and out in the course of their duties. And there was a Cornelius Dola-bella, one of Octavian's followers, who had, she knew, a certain tenderness for her. He was not quite to be trusted, being a Roman, but she felt he would not betray her outright.

By means of these and other friends, she secretly managed to arrange for Caesarion to go to Ethiopia in the company of his tutor. From there they were to escape by ship for India.

With Caesarion out of Octavian's power, she felt a little easier in her mind.

"For surely," she said to Charmion, "the rest are too young to be feared? If he needn't fear them, surely he will spare them? He's ruthless enough, but not vindictive, I think. No, I think there is some hope for my children once *I* am out of the way."

While she still hesitated to take that last fatal step, there came, via her slaves, a message that a body of rebels in the city of Heracleopolis were preparing to rise against the Romans for her sake. By a very ancient tradition, Heracleopolis was sup-posed one day to produce a hero, who would arise to free Egypt from the rule of foreigners. Was this ancient prophecy to be fulfilled at last? She was sorely tempted to believe it, and to give the rebels her secret blessing. For days she brooded over the chance of rescue.

But there was in her nature a strong bedrock of realism and common sense, long submerged in the high-floods of her ambitions. It stood high and dry again now.

"No", was the message she finally managed to smuggle out to the rebels. "I will have no more bloodshed for my sake. If Rome defeats you, Egypt would be destroyed. I will not have Egypt destroyed for the sake of my own life and crown."

She heard no more rumours of rebellions.

Soon after this she learned from her young Roman admirer that Octavian planned to leave for Syria any time now, and that she and her children were to be sent on ahead to Rome, within three days.

"You see? He means us *all* to walk in his Triumph! I can do nothing for my children. And do you think I could bear to see *them* humiliated, any more than I could endure it myself?" said Cleopatra. And a certain scheme, long completed in her mind, was now set into motion.

First she must pay a final visit to Antony's tomb: permission to do so was graciously given by Octavian, and an armed guard arranged.

She had not yet begun to think of Antony as a dead man, and spoke aloud at the tomb as if he could still hear and suffer with her.

"Oh, my dear, dear love!" she mourned. "These are the last offerings you will have from your Cleopatra. I am to be taken far away. Nothing could part us while you lived. But now you must lie here in an Egyptian tomb while I am to go to your country. Oh, Antony! Nothing, in all our misfortunes, was ever so miserable as this last month has been, parted from you. Oh my dear love! Speak for me to the gods who dwell where you are now. Beg them not to abandon your faithful, broken-hearted wife! Beg them not to let her be led in shame through the streets of Rome!"

Unlike Octavian, Cleopatra had never been able to keep her emotions and her politics entirely separate.

Genuinely and bitterly, she grieved for her dead Antony. But this speech was also partly a show, designed to trick Octavian into thinking she was resigned to her fate, that she would submit to being exhibited in his Triumph, and that she had given up all idea of suicide.

Having made the speech in ringing tones which could not fail to be heard and reported, she laid on the tomb garlands of late summer flowers: rose-pink tassels of tamarisk, fragrant white jasmin, and some sweet blue lotus buds. Returning then to the palace, she gave orders for a bath to be prepared.

"For," as she said to Charmion, "I'll not have my body discovered foul after my death, nor put any of you to the disagreeable task of washing a corpse."

Cleansed and rubbed all over with scented oils, she sat down to an excellent supper, to which she brought an excellent appetite, though Charmion and Iras were hardly able to swallow a mouthful.

The dessert was just being passed round, when they heard the guards at the door challenging someone, and laughing over it. Then the door was flung open.

"Right you are, take it in then, old fellow!" said one of the guards. And the head gardener came in with a basket of figs which he placed at Cleopatra's feet.

"A gift from your physician, my lady. Sorry they're a little late," he said. And there was an odd note in his gruff voice which told Cleopatra at once what else was in that basket.

She must give no sign of any such recognition however. Epaphroditus as usual was present at her meal, to make sure that she did not try to defraud Octavian by poisoned food.

"No! No! Not too late. Just in time," she told the old gardener, smiling graciously, and selected one of the figs, which were freshly picked and beautifully ripened.

"Delicious!" she said as she bit into it, and held out the basket invitingly to Epaphroditus. He smilingly shook his head.

Charmion and Iras also refused, looking so distraught as they did so that she was afraid they had betrayed the whole thing.

Calmly she finished her fig, and a second and third one, then, yawning, rose from her chair.

"I'm surprisingly tired tonight. I shall go to bed early. Bring the figs to my bedroom. I may eat one or two more presently," she said. But before she went she produced a sealed letter from the folds of her clothing and gave it to Epaphroditus.

"I wonder if you would be kind enough to have that delivered to Octavian sometime? No hurry!" she said, with one of her most bewitching looks, more impossible to deny than the haughtiest of commands.

Epaphroditus, a little dubiously, agreed.

In her bedroom, the only place in the world where she could now be private (and even so the door was guarded day and night) Cleopatra cautiously lifted up the remaining figs and their cover of fig-leaves.

A small blackish-green creature, coiled in the bottom of the basket, peered up at her, out of the top of its triangular head, from a pair of shining, horny, incredibly ancient-looking eyes, and flickered its tongue at her like a fine thread of smoke.

A responsive flicker of fear shot through her spine at the sight, which she beat out immediately.

"So there you are!" she managed to say with a smile. "Good. I knew Olympus wouldn't fail me."

"Oh, my lady! My lady! How will you find the courage?" whispered Charmion, so pale she might have been the victim herself.

"I must find the courage, Charmion!" said Cleopatra. "And so I *shall*. Come now! Let's get to work. I mean to do the thing in style you know."

So Iras sat down with her mistress at the little silver dressing-box, and set to work to make up her face in the fashion, based on ancient Egyptian styles, which Cleopatra used for her public appearances. She heavily darkened the eyelids with kohl, and exaggerated the size of the eyes by a heavy almond-shaped outline. The eyebrows she plucked and darkened into a pair of slanted wings. Cheeks and lips were brightened with red ochre, the palms of her hands and feet rubbed with henna, and finger and toe-nails painted with the same colour.

All this to her satisfaction, she dipped into a new jar of perfume Cleopatra's best little scent-spoon, with the handle carved like the cat-goddess, and dripped the sweet oil over her temples and hair, ears and throat, and under her arms.

In the meantime Charmion had spread the bed with a cover of woven gold. It would not be comfortable to die on, but for public occasions one must sacrifice comfort for splendour.

Now she came to help Iras. Together they robed Cleopatra in her Isis garments of greenish-blue pleated silk, transparent as shallow sea-water, the low hip girdle embroidered with emeralds, and the collar, as deep as a cape, studded with glittering emeralds, pearls and sapphires.

They brought the ceremonial wig with its myriad jewelled ringlets, which had so bewitched the elderly eyes of Caesar. And finally, in a solemn, sacrificial silence, Charmion placed on top of this the jewelled circlet with the golden serpent rearing at the front, the emblem of Egyptian royalty from time immemorial.

Thus crowned, Cleopatra arranged herself carefully on the bed, and they brought to her, out of its case of soft leather, her best bronze mirror with the handle shaped like the goddess Hathor. She surveyed herself critically as they moved it slowly from her head to her waist.

"Yes. Thank you, Iras. I shall do well enough," she said at last, and found herself for the twentieth time in the midst of a huge yawn. Could it be nerves that were making her so heavy? Or could it be . . . she glanced into the still only partly eaten basket of figs. Could Olympus have added some drug to those figs, to ease her ordeal?

"Oh madam, you look beautiful!" Iras sobbed, streaming with tears now that there was nothing more for her to do. "And so young! Not a day older than when you were our Princess."

Her mistress made a face. "A good many wrinkles older, I'm

afraid, Iras! But not so bad for thirty-nine perhaps!" She sighed. "Ah well, I gave the Romans a run for their money. That's more than some of their other enemies can boast. And now . . . bring me the basket, Charmion—and don't cry! What is there to cry about?"

She took out the rest of the figs in two handfuls, and gave them to the two women, stared down at the coiled creature in the basket for one long steady moment, then snatched it out by the neck, and without further hesitation, without even closing her eyes, clapped it to her upper arm. The two women drew in their breath audibly, but there was no more than a sharp double prick, and then no other immediate pain or effect.

. She replaced the small wriggling body in its basket and lay back with her neck carefully on the wooden neck-rest, so as not to disarrange her wig and crown.

"Stay with me to the end, Charmion," she said calmly, "and if there are unseemly convulsions, put my dress to rights before anyone sees me. I couldn't bear to die in disorder."

For some time there was silence in the room, broken only by Iras's stifled sobs. Charmion had covered her face with her hands, but made no sound.

Presently Cleopatra fancied she could detect not only an increase in her drowsiness, but also a peculiar blurring of her sight, and an abnormal weight in her limbs. With an effort she opened her eyes very wide and looked at Charmion, who seemed suddenly much further away, though she hadn't moved a step.

"Charmion," said Cleopatra, fighting against an unpleasant thickness of tongue and lip, "you've been such a good friend to me. All my life. I don't think I could have endured my life without you. It's so lonely being a Queen. I want you to know how I've valued your love and your loyalty and how much I've loved you. I've left you something—in my will. Not to pay you. I couldn't pay you for what you are. But just to show you how I . . . And you too, Iras: so much more than a waiting-maid. I've left you something too."

"Oh madam ! We shan't want anything !

"Oh my lady, do you think we shall let you go alone?"

Both women were now weeping frantically though still quietly, for fear of the guards just outside the door. But Cleopatra did not hear. Her senses misted over. In a few moments she was gone, well on her way along the road that led to the Country of the West.

THE LETTER which Epaphroditus had been asked to deliver to Octavian contained a request that when Cleopatra was dead, she should be buried with Mark Antony in her own mausoleum.

Octavian read the message in secret satisfaction, knowing very well what his captive must be up to.

Cleopatra alive was something of an embarrassment. Not that he had to fear much direct harm from her now Antony was dead. But she could still be the focus of Egyptian unrest. His spies had not failed to report symptoms of that in Heracleopolis and other towns up the Nile.

A Cleopatra murdered might be a still more dangerous focus for insurrection. He could not afford to have her publicly executed, or even privately disposed of in any way that would throw suspicion on himself.

But a Cleopatra dead by her own hand was quite another matter, especially if it looked as if he had tried to prevent the suicide.

So he delayed for some time after receiving her letter, and then bustled off his men with orders to, "Look sharp about it," hoping they wouldn't look *too* sharp.

They managed it very nicely.

When the guards burst open her bedroom door, they found the Queen lying in all her splendour on her bed of gold, quite dead.

Iras lay across her feet, all but dead too. And Charmion, her eyes clouded, scarcely able to hold up her head, was kneeling at the top of the bed, trying to re-arrange the crown, which was perfectly straight in any case. Cleopatra had died peacefully with no disturbance to her dignity whatever.

"This is a dirty trick of your lady's!" shouted one of the guards as he strode up to the bed.

"No! A splendid deed, worthy of the Queen. Oh! She was rare, she was brave, was my Princess!" murmured Charmion. Then she too fell across the Queen's body and was dead before they could bring help to her.

On the floor in the empty fig basket lay the small dark snake with the bulging neck, living replica of the golden one that crowned the forehead of the last of the Pharaohs of Egypt.

Octavian gave Cleopatra a very handsome funeral. He could well afford it with all the treasure of Egypt now at his command. She was buried as she had desired, beside the body of the man who had walked hand in hand with her to their mutual ruin.

Not long after the funeral, Antyllus, Antony's eldest boy, aged seventeen, was put to death by Octavian's orders.

So was Caesarion. The tutor to whom his mother had trusted him had treacherously made him come back before ever reach-into Ethiopia, saying that Octavian was going to make him King of Egypt.

The three younger children were sent to Rome to be looked after by Octavia, who seemed to regard her home as an orphanage for all Antony's progeny.

History does not tell us what happened to the two little boys, or even whether they ever grew up. Cleopatra "the Moon" was in due course given in marriage to Juba, King of part of North Africa. Nothing much more is known of her either.

Her children dead or powerless nonentities, her beloved Egypt the personal property of the man who was shortly to be the first Roman Emperor, Cleopatra might as well never have been born, for all she had achieved.

Yet it is clear that in contemporary eyes she was a woman to be reckoned with: a woman of great ability and intelligence, as well as tremendously vital and charming, no negligible figure even to the most formidable of the Romans.

Her character has come down to us mainly through the distorting mirror of Octavian's war-propaganda. There are few reliable documents. Plutarch's account of her is thought to be both biased and romanticised.

Even so, of all the personalities of those turbulent years, hers is among the few that stand out. Amongst her family, the Ptolemies, her name is the only one most people have even heard of. In fact, out of all the thirty centuries of Egyptian history, is there any name so generally well-known as hers?

Cleopatra has become a legend. There are, after all, not many people, particularly women, to whom this has happened.

A Bibliography

A History of Egypt, J. H. Breasted
The Cambridge Ancient History, Vols 6, 7 and 10
Strabo, Book 17
Plutarch's Lives, Vols 2 and 3
The Splendour That Was Egypt, Margaret A. Murray
Egypt, Leonard Cottrell
Ancient Egypt, Hermann Kees
Everyday Life in Ancient Egypt, John Manchip White
Daily Life In Roman Egypt, Jack Lindsay
From the Grachi to Nero, H. H. Scullard, FBA, FSA
Roman Women, J. P. V. D. Balsdon
Social Life At Rome in the Age of Cicero, W. Warde Fowler